the
GAME
MASTER'S
GAMBIT

Jeff Babineaux

Published 2015 by Jeff Babineaux
PO Box 4781, Shreveport, LA 71134
Book design and cover by Lia Rees at Free Your Words
(www.freeyourwords.com)
Fonts used: Akoom, Aleo, WC Mano Negra, BlackJack, Electra

ISBN: 978-0692418840

Dedication

Lia, you understand me only through words I have written. What more could a writer ask?

Mango, you stoked the fires of creativity and begged for more when I handed you a manuscript I thought was complete.

Melody, you are my first and most important pair of eyes. I am blind and lost without you.

Finally, Reader. Yes, you. This book is dedicated to you if, upon finishing, you find a game that excites you, throw out the rule book, and make memories with what's left in the box.

Contents

ZERO

A tiny hand reached for purchase, grabbing onto the smallest rocks that jutted from the castle's massive stone walls. The walls had aged to deep dark black, coated in the soot of wildfires that swept the countryside. It felt gritty on her hands. By now they were so coated in ash that her black palms stood dark against the pale back of her hands. Her ball gown was ripped and torn from the climb, coming to tatters about her short little legs. She had been climbing for an hour, and she was still only halfway up the tower.

She had traveled far on the wise priestess' words. The magical crown that could restore the kingdom was stolen, and the only way to get it back was if she herself, the young crown princess of the Rose Kingdom, retrieved it from the dragon's lair. She enlisted no aid, and she took every precaution to stay hidden on the roads along the way, because this was no place for a ten-year-old girl.

Her long dark hair, filled with twigs from the black forest, fell behind her. Drying mud from the haunted bogs caked her feet. She was a tattered mess, but her year-long journey was finally coming to an end. The setting sun dipped behind her as she put a hand over the only window on the great tower. Within, she could see the crimson tapestries lining the walls. She rolled over the edge of the window sill and onto the lush carpet, coming up to face the black dragon eating the bones of the last hero to attempt to scale the tower.

"No. I don't like that." Caro peeked out from under her covers as her father sat at her bedside. "No scary stuff, you promised!"

"You're right honey. I promised."

The princess rolled on the plush carpet to find a towering, pink dragon baking a new batch of cookies, her last dozen strewn about the floor all around them. "Well, well, well. What have we got here? A princess? My, I thought my day was as interesting as it was going to get. Well, Princess, what have you to say for yourself?"

"DIE, DRAGON!"

"Are you sure, honey?" Her father looked on sleepily as she came out from under her covers, arms raised and shouting triumphantly in the dead of night. "Die, dragon? You could ground him, or tell him to go away, or talk about the magic crown you made me spend two days drawing and describing. Last I remember, didn't the crown magically make tea?"

"Yes," she nodded matter-of-factly. "Tea, dresses, and rainbows. The dragon is bad, right? So I can stab him?"

"Um, with your sword?"

"Uh huh."

The princess remembered that she had a sword and pulled it out from her tattered dress, squaring off with the dragon. The dragon let out a mighty roar, shooting flames across the room, and the princess rolled away to dodge them. She charged in closer, great sword dragging behind her because it was so heavy she could barely lift it.

She jumped into the air and thrust the sword at the mighty dragon, but the winged devil grabbed the sword from her, tucking it under its massive, scaly arms. It let out a loud cry of pain, throwing its free hand in the air as if to say "Why?!?!" and then slumped to the ground.

"Is it dead?"

"Of course not honey. It's the middle of the night. The dragon is sleeping, just like Daddy wishes he was."

"Oh, good. Tell me about the crown!"

The crown glittered gold in the deep dark of the room, lighting her way to a hidden stairway that could take her back to her kingdom. When she came back triumphant, wearing her crown, the curse cast on the townspeople lifted and everyone was happy again. The End.

"Yay!"

"Mmmhmm. Okay, honey. Now it's time to go to bed. Daddy's gotta work in the morning." Her father's stubble scratched against the pillow cases as he lay half-awake, struggling to stay alert in the late hour.

Caro pouted, twisting the red dragon covers in her hands as she pulled them over her shoulders, getting settled in. "Not yet. Do the thing again."

"The thing?"

"Yeah. It's not The End until you do the thing!"

"The... oooh." The revelation was sudden. "You're right, honey. How could I forget experience points? Well, let's see: you saved the kingdom, defeated the dragon and climbed the tower. That's gotta be, like, 24 million. You were at level 263 before, so Princess Caro is now at level 271."

"Yay!" She giggled and pulled her pillow in closer to her head.

"Are you going to go to sleep now?"

Her eyes were already heavy. He turned off her white knight lamp, turned on her wizard's crystal ball night light, and kissed her on her forehead. "See you in the morning, Princess."

"Good night, Daddy."

TEN YEARS LATER

Caro's alarm buzzed loudly in her ear. She hit the snooze roughly. One of these days, the alarm clock would break and she'd go back to using her phone. She was less likely to break the phone. Even her sleeping brain was alert enough to be careful with nice things.

Her room was a mess. She planned to clean it last night, but the impending graduation weighed too heavily on her, and so she resorted to procrastination. More and more, when difficult choices came to mind, she would just freeze and wish them all away. It hadn't worked yet.

She dug through a basket of clean clothes, and came up with a pair of green denim jeans and a baggy Midnight Syndicate shirt that swallowed her slim frame. She brushed her chin-length hair out of her face and surveyed the remains of her clean laundry basket: a pink shirt that she wore when she ran out of options last week and three socks that didn't match. She would do laundry tonight. Perhaps the monotony of getting things done would ease the pain of what she had to do this afternoon. She was days away from graduation, and there were so many goodbyes to say before the season of endings would be over. There was the gaming group, whom she would miss dearly, but they by and large seemed to understand, and then there was Christopher.

Christopher had been her closest ally and greatest confidant through all of the mess of high school years. He stood by her through her father's cancer, and spoke for her when she couldn't at the funeral. He was a good guy, but he was perfectly fine staying where he was. She tripped over one of his t-shirts, one that she had bought for him at a G-Love concert that he had been so excited about. She tossed it into a box with his name scrawled along one side and moved into the bathroom to brush her teeth. Caro needed more, and she knew she couldn't motivate him or be okay with his laziness. She would find a way to tell him how she felt today, and then she would walk away and never look back.

She would find a way to let him know, at least. She didn't think she could look him in the eye and tell him that she wouldn't be hanging on to him when she left. He would find someone else. Maybe some pizza delivery girl who loved living just below the poverty level. High school made their friendship easy, and their long friendship made their heated and contentious relationship feel natural. She just didn't want to go through all of that with a full plate of engineering work ahead of her.

She threw her sketchbook, bag of dice, and her laptop into a backpack and headed for the car. She pretended she might do some more online research about north Louisiana, but she doubted she would be doing much with thoughts of Christopher and her father's death on her mind. "Optimism will carry the day," she kept telling herself, and so she jumped in the car and headed to the one place she could escape from every other distraction, be with her thoughts. She went to the library.

ONE

Caro sat huddled in one corner of the library, hiding under headphones and listening to Final Fantasy music. She crumpled the paper she had scribbled on, sure the crinkling could be heard throughout the library. She tried to separate herself from the task at hand while trying to be genuine with her decision and follow-through. She took her gel pen in hand, and started scribbling on the fresh sheet of flowery stationery. If she had to do it on paper, she might as well make it expensive paper.

Dear Christopher,

You must have known this day was coming. I did everything I could to show you the signs—

She scratched through the lines, balled up the paper and threw it on the carpet next to her. He deserved to know, he had to have seen it coming, but pointing that out now seemed against everyone's best interests. She started anew, writing in big, flowing letters, trying to feel as loving as possible.

My Dearest Chris,

My journey begins anew in a few short weeks, and that journey must be without you—

She palmed the pad of stationery, looked up as it crumpled in her hands. The tears in her eyes blurred the clock on the wall. She started with the basics, reminding him how much she loved him. She loved him, after all. She loved him as much as any high school girl could. In fact, none of them could love as fiercely as she did. She'd told him about college time and again, with his repeated shrugs, brushing aside her future plans as he rose up the ranks at the local pizza store. He would be manager soon. He had already worked his way up to shift lead in just two years.

"Smooth sailing," he used to tell her. It was his way of telling her it would all be all right, but every time she heard him say it, she pictured him on a sailboat, feet propped up, sails popping, quite literally, going wherever the wind blew him. To Chris it was probably a lot like drifting down river and calling it progress. He knew that the wind was blowing, and that he was moving. He tried to convince her how she wouldn't have to work once he got promoted to management.

She never considered staying, and he never asked. Now, just 15 days from moving day, she was getting ready to leave and he still didn't seem interested in her goals and dreams. But in refusing to see her life away from her family home, he had cut his own rope. She would have taken her with him, if only he could dream of a better life than fast food hell. She wanted more. She couldn't imagine a life with a man who didn't. She looked at the books on the shelves surrounding her. The genealogy section was always her favorite: stories upon stories of families (the tales of where they went, how they lived, and a line that seemed to always run into the future from the distant past). The old and dusty shelves fit her mood. This crypt of abandoned library space was where she always came when the tension mounted and she just wanted out. If she couldn't escape to her dream world, she could at least escape to history.

Hidden behind these stacks of history, she was safe from the present. Very few people passed through this section of the library. Here among the deepest and richest history of her small town, she was safe from the patrons that never made it past the Twilight books and computers. She worked at the end of her pen with her teeth, biting nervously. She felt secluded here, just a few short steps past the computer bank where regulars wasted an hour at a time on Facebook games and YouTube videos. People needed so much help to play inside their heads.

Her letter composed itself after that. Christopher was always a Facebook gamer, too ready to get caught up in the daily drama of social games and keeping in touch with painfully casual acquaintances. She was sorry to be leaving him, but he would find solace in the next pretty face. She folded her letter and then took out her pencils to sketch.

There was something wholly freeing about drawing her stories and worlds on vellum paper. The devil-may-care way she could scribble fleeting thoughts and worlds onto a fifty-cent page made every stroke of the pencil more precious, made every dungeon and map more real. She drew a journey, imagining her life as she crossed hundreds of miles of forest and swamp as a stranger in an undiscovered country. She dreaded the thought of being the new girl so far from the lifetime of friendships and connections she grew up in, but the adventure of making a new life for herself in that distant world excited her. She imagined the perils on the road, and the evil city that stood in her way.

Her thoughts wandered to the bricks laid of energy-draining powers that would make even the simplest of movement a heroic task. The vampiric professors that thrived on her thirst for knowledge would no doubt make every attempt to drain her dry before the course of her studies were through, but the degree like a dragon's hoard would sustain her for the rest of her life.

Here in her home village, a simple life was all that was afforded to even the bravest of warriors. She learned what magic she could from the elementary wizards who tutored her, but her fires fizzled and her ice rays were lukewarm at best. Her husband, the mighty giant, spent most of his days in slumber, wasting his energy as the town starved from lack of food. With a great swoop of his claws, he could till the soil that would feed the farmers. His mighty back could bear the weight of valuable stone which would fortify their walls. Instead, he only slept.

This savior of the village would do them no good. It was up to her, but her measly powers would prove no great value. She needed a great tutor, and no good wizard could be found in their small village. She would venture far to the north, through the bogs of gloom and past the thickets of rage. The trees and vines would block her path, but she would not falter. She pictured the halls of the wizardry school, adorned with pictures of the mighty heroes who had grown in power from the great wizard's tutelage.

None had names yet. She hated giving names to something she had never seen. One by one, though, the players took the stage. Her paper filled with glorious robes, gilded with gold and woven in magic. The vampires each had their own heraldry, with altars weaving tales of their exploits. One had the slaughter of a dozen villages mashed together into a cacophonous display of blood and shadow. Another depicted a wizard taming a tarrasque, the mightiest of beasts, and kingdoms bowed before him. The great dragon at the top of the highest tower sat on a mound of gold, jewels and scrolls, a testament to the knowledge, power and wealth that she hoped she'd win for herself. Her giant would never have any of it, would never follow her. She would venture alone, and find what allies she could along the way.

She put his letter in an envelope and sealed it before walking out of the library. She would spend the better part of the day writing out an adventure to walk herself through when she missed game night. She mused through these scenarios, occasionally rolling dice to keep things a little random. It wasn't as much fun as it was in a group, but it would have to do until she made more friends.

How was she supposed to make friends? She pondered the difficulty outside the library. The warm August air tossed her hair in swirls as she made her way to the rust-red Nissan Sentra in the parking lot. The same heap that helped her through her high school years working at the game store was going to have to do while she was "up North." She was fully aware of the irony of referring to northern Louisiana as Yankee country, but preferred to refer that way to everything north of I-10 as such. She heard tales of people visiting "up North" all littered with unkind people. People "up North" didn't smile when you made eye contact with them. People "up North" didn't invite you to have dinner with the family when you were on your own. People "up North," through all of the stories passed in her circles, didn't spend much time doing anything other than asking questions about the pet alligators, pirogues and bare feet of the people "down South."

Making conversation would be hard enough. She could picture no scenario where she met someone who shared her love of gaming, fantasy worlds and stories, and could hold a conversation. She pictured the southern warmth missing from their faces, and how much harder it might be to break through their ice when she struggled to connect with a group of people well-known for social awkwardness.

Chris was none of those. Like so many friends in high school, Chris was just there at the right time. It was easy to get his attention, and he was kind enough when it counted. From now on, she supposed friends would be harder to come by. Her lips curled into a half-smile before her face hardened as she steeled herself. She wished she could have some of that Yankee emotional disconnect as she drove over to Christopher's house.

She pulled up to the house a little before 5. He wouldn't get off work for another hour, and she wanted to slip the note through the bedroom window and slip away unnoticed. She rounded the corner of the white ranch home, working her way around the black shutters and in between the kitchen and garage to his window on the back side of the house. The empty house felt like a small blessing. His family had started to feel like her own, and she didn't want to have to say goodbye to them.

His black window sill sat about shoulder height to her, so she stepped on her tip toes to push the window up. She put the note where she always put them, at the edge of his desk, so that it stuck partially out onto the back yard. She smiled when she imagined one of her notes getting partially soaked by a rain storm before he realized it was there. Things that were out of place could take days for him to find. Then again, if she didn't leave a note it might take longer for him to realize that she was gone.

As she jumped to pull the window down, she heard a car engine pulling up the driveway. How did he get off work so early? She listened from around the corner of the house as the car door opened blasting Led Zeppelin, which finally cut off as he took the keys out of the ignition. She walked gingerly up to the corner, hoping that he wouldn't notice her. She hid behind old wood that piled up from the garage wall project that Chris said he would finish someday. She could see the front corner of his maroon Taurus as its door slammed shut in a thud of rickety metal and aging plastic. If she could just sneak past as he went around the car…

Chris stood from the driver's seat, his black shirt crusted with a mixture of water and dough and pizza sauce. He fumbled with the keys in his hand, a lit cigarette in his mouth. He turned to walk toward the house when a receipt fell out of his hand, floating to the ground. He shambled to the front of the car to grab it, and saw Caro, who felt strangely like a prowler lurking in the bushes.

His tired eyes lit up slightly. "Hey, babe. There you are. What you doing on this end of town?"

Caro flushed. She hoped she could steer him inside and walk away. "Oh, just checking in on my way to see Dad." It was a go-to excuse for her on tough days. When she was inconsolable, when she got depressed and didn't want to be cheered up, or when she just genuinely wanted to be left alone, she always told him she was going to visit her father.

Chris processed the news. "Checking in on me? Lucky I got off early. I might not've gotten to see you today." Yep. Lucky you. Chris looked at the ground, chasing the receipt before making his way to the door. He didn't even look back when he asked, "Are you coming in?"

Caro laid a hand on the side of the house, one foot on the driveway as she balked, "I – I don't think so. I'd better go." Chris paused. "I should get going. One of those days." She frowned as he turned to look at her for the second time today.

"Did you leave me a note?" His eyes lit up counting the days since she had left one, and he smiled as he picked up the pace toward the door. "You did, didn't you?"

Caro began to blush. She was getting choked up, and couldn't speak. No matter what she said, he would bubble over with mush. His eyes were half on her, half on the search for a love letter that she knew he wasn't going to like. He grabbed her by the hand. "Come on, babe. It's been a terrible day. Mike left early and I had to cover his shift on dishes." That explained the smell at least. "With everything going on at the store, I just haven't had a whole lot of time for us. All that's going to change really soon..." She opened her mouth, but only stuttered. He still wasn't getting it. He must have attributed the pain he saw on her face to her need to visit her father, so he pressed on, smiling warmly. "Pretty soon, they say we'll have enough employees that I can have every other weekend off."

"I'm breaking up with you." They were past the kitchen, at the doorway to his bedroom. The words spilled out of her mouth. She couldn't think of any reason to hold back any longer. Her slumbering giant was steps away from the letter that said it all, and she figured maybe if she told him it would soften the blow... maybe not today, but in the long run.

Chris picked up the squared letter from the window sill and traced the contour of its sharp, pristine edges. Caro looked down and opened her mouth, letting out low whispers and backtracking out of 'it's not you, it's me,' or 'I just need some space' as Chris creased the letter over again in his hands, folding it one more time before tossing it unread onto the bed. "I don't get it. I try so hard."

She tried to say that they grew apart, and that she still loved him, but not in the same way. She wished she could tell him she really wanted to break up, but it wasn't perfectly true. At least, not true enough for what he deserved. Her sweet, pitiful Chris deserved to be doted over by a small town girl. He was kind, and that had been everything to her once. She imagined him down the road, talking about how he did everything he could, and she still walked away. He hadn't done everything he could, though. Could she really say, after all the good and bad years, that he had ever fought for her?

"What do you think it means to try, Christopher?" As the words came out of her mouth, they sounded cold and heartless. "Was it 'trying' when you passed up game nights to switch to a dead end job because you liked getting driver tips at night? Sure. But what were you 'trying' for?"

Chris started to cry. She figured there would be plenty of time once she got out of here to cry. She would have to push through. "How hard were you 'trying,' Chris, when you gave up on college because I was a year behind you in school? Was that 'trying?' Now that I'm going, why are you staying now?"

"Things are finally picking up for me here. You don't see that. You don't see me trying. You don't see that I love you." He looked like he might fight to keep her, might argue all night, but then he dropped his hands to his side. "Everything I did, I did for us," he insisted. She knew that he believed that. She knew that he thought of them as some sort of couple that might make do with the little jobs that were everywhere here in their home town. It burned her up that he was so sure that she would give up on college just because he had. He was sure that she would wallow in mediocrity, because he would.

"The 'us' that you imagine isn't real. I'm sorry." When his face twisted further into ugly crying she decided it was time to go. He'll figure it out. He'll find his own way. No doubt if he did, he might tell her how he was doing it for her, but she wouldn't want to go back once her future began. Still, hopefully his next relationship would be stronger, hopefully her lovable giant would make a future that she would be proud of. She locked the door for him on the way out, hoping despite everything that he would be okay for the night, because her grand adventure stretched out before her.

As her Nissan pulled out of the drive, she turned south, out of town. All of this change made her miss the greatest constant in her life. Perhaps she would go to her dad after all. The lights of the city fell away behind her as she turned onto a parish road toward a small community with only an abandoned church, a handful of trailers and a graveyard.

The smell of fresh-cut grass hit her as she stepped out of the car. The graveyard grew in leaps and bounds in the four years that Caro had been coming here. Graves popped up all around her father's headstone, marking the time like rings around the trunk of a tree.

The short stone bench that once sat like a theater seat in front of a single grave became the center of attention of many more marble markers, fanning out until she felt as if she were in the middle of some kind of Stonehenge. The years were kind to the marble etching on the headstone. Shiny lacquer still shone in the dark lettering. It still seemed fresh and new, like the wounds left gaping from the father who died too soon.

An older man with fair wisps of red hair sat at one end of a concrete bench. He seemed to get younger every time she saw him. Perhaps she just felt more grown up today than usual.

"Heya, Pops." She sat on the other side of the bench, hanging her messenger bag over her lap and fidgeting with the clasp.

"Heya, yourself." Her father stared straight through her, smiling the way he would when she would make up stories for him, and then looked back to his grave. She struggled to remember any other face he ever made, and those emotions that she remembered seemed to dwindle every year. "How's your mother?"

"Oh, you know… always working." She reached out to grab his hand, but he didn't move. "She says she might come visit soon."

"You don't have to try to cheer me up, Princess." He looked down at the grass at his feet. "Your mother only comes when you drag her here. That's fine by me. They all say I'm in a better place, so why should it matter to me?"

Caro sighed, standing up and walking up to the headstone. She half-kneeled, running her fingers across the smooth marble. "It matters to me. No matter where you are, this is where I find you best." Dirt clumped on the dulling marble. It felt gritty against her skin. "They really should take better care of you here."

"Don't be ridiculous, Princess. I don't get why you still come here anymore. You have always had memories of us at home, picnics, and gaming conventions. Any day, any hour, any minute in that big head of yours, you have a trove of happy memories and pleasant scenes, yet you still come down here four, five times a year just to see this sad place."

"It's not sad here," Caro smiled. She turned to see him still on the bench. "This place is more than just a memory. It's tangible."

"You should be out living your life. You should be half way to Cancun, making good use of the money I left you. I left that money so you could make your own life, instead of living in the past with the things that I left behind. Besides, since when does my little Princess need something tangible? Aren't you a little old for blankies, binkies and… marble headstones? You're leaving home. You don't need physical things to hang onto anymore."

"Dad, it's not like that. I promise." He just shrugged. Caro sat across his lap and she felt like a young girl again. "I need to get out of here, sure, but I'll never really be gone. This is the plan I've been making for years. I always wanted to follow in your footsteps. This place, Mom, and home – it grounds me."

"Yes, well, this place grounds me, too," her father replied. "About six feet." Caro rolled her eyes. No matter how long gone her father was, his humor would spring eternal.

"See? I still need you. I still need your Dad jokes." He didn't seem so certain, but she continued, "Mom doesn't tell them right. Bless her heart, she tries."

"Of course she does. I don't know how she makes the time. She works so hard."

Caro just shrugged. Her mother spent very little time at home, and most of that time was spent just trying to keep things going around the house. She would come home from work exhausted, clean things that Caro had just cleaned, and then cook meals for the next day so her little baby girl wouldn't starve. Caro tried cooking for herself, but her mother always turned up her nose, insisting that Caro would die of malnutrition had she been left to her own devices.

"That's not why I came to talk, anyway."

"Oh?"

"It's Chris." Caro took a deep breath. "We broke up today."

In a breath, her father was standing in front of her in vintage boxing gloves and helmet and awful shorts. "Did he hurt my baby girl? Let me at'em. I'll murdalize him."

Caro laughed breathily and rolled her eyes. "It was the other way around, Daddy. I hurt him."

"Fine by me," her father relaxed, slipping back into his dad jeans and old t-shirt. "He never deserved my princess, anyway."

"Whatever. You would have liked him. He was kind." She tried to think of a single time that Chris was mean to her, but none came to mind. "He just wasn't ready for the kind of life that I'm headed for. I mean, you were always driven, just like Mom, and I've seen what that does to even you two."

Her father had been an engineer. Not just some corporate engineer that came home every day at 5, but the kind that took frequent trips to crazy, amazing places because they needed him. She had loved to hear his stories of South America, of Mexico and the exotic locales. She loved him for what he had done for them, by providing for her future as he jetted off to far away jobs all over the world, but she also saw the toll it took on her parents' relationship. The college fund that he left behind when he passed was too much, more than double what she would spend at a decent college, and she gladly would have given it up if it would have spared some of the stress from him being gone all the time.

Caro's mother was a researcher in a local bio lab. She frequently worked late, and never changed her schedule on the precious few days that Dad would be home. Caro's parents put up a good front, but the cold tension on the few meals that they were able to share was palpable. She tried to talk Caro into going into her field, insisting that she would have a knack for biology, but Caro dreaded the possibility of being holed up in a laboratory. After Dad's death, Mom seemed to give in to the workload, and Caro figured if she was going to work eighty hours every week, she should at least get to spend some of those days in fun and new places.

"I'm sorry," Caro shrugged away the old memories. "I didn't mean to bring it up. I just, I can't imagine Chris–" She looked up and he was gone. Maybe it was a defense mechanism for her. She wasn't sure why he would leave her when she started feeling like this. It kept her from seeing him angry, at least. She reached into her pocket and pulled out a penny, placing it on top of the grave before heading back to the car. The rest of the pennies had disappeared. They always did around the beginning of summer. They were meant for her father, there was some superstition that it would bring him good fortune in the afterlife. She used to pretend that he came to pick them up personally. She figured whether it was him or some neighborhood kids, he still got the good fortune in the long run.

She got back in the car and started the engine. One more session with the old group, and then Mom would bring her up to college and get her settled in. She felt lucky – it was the first vacation her mother had taken in years, and they would be spending it moving boxes into a cramped dorm room. She supposed it was the only way she could get Mom to take a day off. She figured she might even get a road trip dinner out of her.

She knew that life would go on without all of this. Still, her mother, this graveyard, and her group were her greatest anchors. She would miss them all equally, she imagined.

TWO

Legends say that evil wizards who amass enough power never have to die. Their dark imaginations and desires drift toward equal parts immortality and the destruction of anything viewed as more powerful. The truly twisted manage to find a compromise of both in the body of a lich.

The lich is the embodiment of the dark desires of these power-mad beings. With centuries added to their life spans, they spend every waking moment in the dried husk of magical undeath dedicated to amassing greater power. The most successful lich can grow strong enough to endanger the fabric of reality itself. When a brave group of heroes seek out such a menace, there is very rarely any indication of the vile being's true power, and never a guarantee that they will make it back alive.

A week's travel south from the Bronze Gates of Farial Kingdom brought just such a group of heroes on a quest to rid the land of a lich rumored to be in possession of a book that could swallow the realm in darkness. In a sepulcher cracked with the ages of moss growing in between and the weight of warriors' feet, they tread as stealthily as they could manage. Dozens showed up over the last three hundred years to face the lich queen in her habitat. Outside of its profane walls, nothing could destroy her permanently. Flaming sconces woofed to life as the band of heroes neared, led by the savage Kitara. Kitara tread lightly, each step silent in front of another. Beneath her scarlet robes, a dozen daggers, darts and wands held an arsenal that could level an entire city. This was the purpose of her life, and she would see it through, even if within it, was her last breath.

The knight, Sir Phteven, followed behind, his brilliant bastard sword lighting the way for the rest of the group whose eyes could not adapt to the near-pitch black ambiance of Castle Riven. His silver armor was bought in blood from the dragon Scevith, whose scales could still be discerned in the largest sections of plate on his massive chest. Sir Phteven paced thirty feet behind, doing his best to keep the magical armor that he wore quiet. From behind him, the twins pushed and shoved to stay out of last place in the death march up to the annihilator lich's main room. Both survived by being lucky enough to never get too far from the great knight, and by alternately taking the brunt of the surprise attacks that invariably came from behind as most of the monsters whose paths they crossed never realized they were there until long after the female assassin had passed.

The scout's keen eyes kept them safe most days, but very rarely could protect them from the evils that hid in shadow, cloaked in invisibility or beneath the deep stones imbued with the magical darkness of the Lich Dark Dugan's hideaway. As an extra precaution, he walked with his bow constantly drawn, prepared to shoot down anything that made a move for the group he had sworn to protect.

The entryway to the Lich's lair lay before them. Kitara pulled her thieves' tools from a lavender pouch and began to work on the magical lock, weaving incantations with dexterity until the massive lock cracked beneath her skill. The party froze, making prayers to each of their gods that the fearsome Dugan would not hear their approach, which would make this epic battle all the more impossible. Kitara nodded to the knight to make the first move. Whatever lay in wait, Phteven would be the most capable to deal with the first wave of carnage that the mighty sorceress could throw at them. As the door creaked open a great shriek could be heard from within, "Welcome, travelers. The next steps will be your last. You have come seeking glory, but all you will find inside is death."

So much for the element of surprise. The twins readied their bows, each commanding a different elemental power and working together to find the best flanking positions. Their cloaks of rushing leaves covered them from nearly every direction, leaving only small areas open that followed the tips of their arrows. They circled the outside of the room as Kitara pushed Phteven forward, following closely behind him.

Dark Dugan sat on her throne of thorns bemoaning the arrival of another distraction. She spent the last fifty years poring over the works of Morrigan the Bard, and finally reached the moment in the requiem movement written in honor of his death where the posthumous ghost writer speaks on the good and bad of his life through his eyes. It was a touching moment for her: the hero's villainous tale of all of his darkest deeds, shone in the light of all the good that he had done. Dugan pictured a world in which the same could be said of her as high strings cried victorious over the deep, melancholy bass. Her most terrible deeds had been so few and far between that she imagined her good deeds might endure. She had, after all, given the map to the Shard of Destiny to a troop of heroes just decades before, and she imagined if she did enough of those, perhaps the souls she sacrificed (including her own) in order to gain immortality could be forgotten or glossed over in the annals of history. What might she do to be viewed as the heroine who was once a villain? Perhaps if she did something good for the distractions interrupting her thoughtful meditations, her name might be spread across the land as Dugan the Dutiful instead…

She considered carefully as the knight in shining armor strode into the main walking area. Seriously? She thought to herself. The stereotype was too strong with this one to do any good. She was sure that he would strike first, loot second, and then never end up asking questions at all. Just behind him, though, was a feral woman, whose darkness in her eyes fascinated the mighty Dugan. How could such a dark beauty join the company of such a stupid, narrow-minded knight? The twins that followed last into the great hall also amused her, bows drawn, and it appeared as if they were waiting for some small movement in the stained glass art or the magical carpets, upon which the foursome would unleash hell. Heroes were funny that way.

Dugan extinguished the magical sconces and brought the lit stones beneath their feet to a dim glow. Everyone started turning around frantically, everyone except the girl with darkness in her eyes. Dugan saw an opportunity: she would be the only one who could see the evil sorceress as Dugan offered a peace sign. Dugan stood before

Kitara, gesturing peacefully as the other three flailed about helplessly. Kitara looked deep into the aged, petrified face of Dugan, searching for a message in the silence.

In the light green glow of Kitara's starlight vision, Dugan proffered open hands and the warmest smile the undead sorceress could offer. The little noise that she made was drowned out by the sounds of a bard's singing in the far corner of the room. Kitara considered the most obvious possibility that the lich was looking for an ally in the darkness. Would she expect the assassin to join the lich in combat against the party of heroes? One less person would certainly tip the scales away from their favor, as they were nearly overpowered with all four against the mighty, ancient monster. An inkling came to mind that the lich wanted no fight at all from the four, but that thought seemed a distant possibility, as Kitara reasoned that it was highly unlikely that the lich would lose a fight in which three of the four had no idea where she was at the beginning. In one fell swoop, the lich could take out all but the fast assassin, and then a one on one fight would prove no difficult feat for Dugan, owing to the fact that Kitara was no match for her face to face.

Dugan motioned to Kitara to stay quiet, and she lowered her daggers. Dugan's body let loose some of its tension, and motioned for her to follow. As Dugan made it to the altar, Kitara stepped up onto the onyx platform and examined the room around them. The twins stood back to back, and one of the bows was aimed squarely for the knight, the noisiest object in the room. The lich opened a great dusty book, and Kitara flipped through its pages, revealing the music and secrets of the long-dead sorceress. Holding her hands up in a gesture *of peace, Dugan smiled at the thought that she might finally have found a way free of the stigma of the undead.*

A blazing, white-hot dagger ripped from under Kitara's robes and struck the underside of the lich's leathery jaw. A small pinprick of gleaming adamantium shone from the crown of the crone's head.

"Direct hit!" Caro shot up from her chair at the table. She did a little dance as the lich toppled on the game map onto its side. The 20 on the 20-sided die lay face up beside the miniatures on the table. She ran a victory lap around the table at the culmination of a year of adventuring with her friends. Jeb looked up from his dungeon master's screen at the paper carnage before him. Caro collected high fives from Jude and Jeremy, the two identical twins, as the twins shouted over each other to see who would loot the body first.

Jeb twisted his face in disgust. "Really, Caro? This is how you want it to go?" Four pages of back story behind the lich they followed for months sat under the page where its health points were tracked, a big red zero being the painful reminder of what happens when players don't want to play along with the storyline. Caro only shrugged, and Jeb shot back, "You could have had it all. The lich had the answers to your character's past, it had access to riches beyond your wildest dreams…" Jeb sighed, lifting his heavy frame from the table. "The assassin plays the short game. You get one fourth of the loot you could have gotten, and your character goes out with an unfortunate fizzle." He grabbed his cane from beside the green matted gaming table as he walked toward the drink table beside the kitchen.

Caro eyed Jeb's disgust, and pouted playfully. "Poor Dungeon Master. I play my way, and we just knocked out a villain we shouldn't be able to take out for another four levels, with the element of surprise on our side despite all efforts to the contrary!" At that, she gestured toward the noisy knight.

Stephen shot back from behind his fort of Mountain Dew cans, "Don't look at me. The dice are trying to kill me. I couldn't roll above a 5 all night." It had been his idea all along to maintain the element of surprise, but that became impossible when the luck ran out on his 20-sided die.

The DM sat dumbfounded and unrelenting, popping the top off of an IBC and grimacing into his drink. Caro grunted in exasperation, "It doesn't have to be your way, Jeb. We had fun!" She chucked his shoulder, trying to draw a smile out of him, "What's the harm in breaking off on our own way once in a while?"

She wasn't wrong, but it still seemed ridiculous to him. After months of preparation, and lots of writing and struggling on his part to create an opportunity for her to go out as a legend, his favorite player was leaving on a sour note of 'kill the monsters, stab your buddy, add up the XP and move on'. He didn't get it, but Caro was sure that he never would. Jeb handed her one of his favorite root beers, his surly expression lightening only a little. "I just tried to make it great. You know, for your last day with us."

Caro sucked her teeth at that. She spent very little time thinking on the days ahead, and her last opportunity at escaping through their weekly gaming sessions was a success, but she knew that the time was approaching quickly, and that this time Saturday, she would be on a bus heading for college, and her friends, family, and everything familiar to her would be left behind. Jeb could see her hesitation on her mind when he held his hands up helplessly. "Why'd you have to do it? We have plenty of good colleges here. There's a great engineering program here at LSU."

Caro shook her head. "Nope. I'm getting out of this place, Jeb. I promise it's not your fault." She pushed her hair back out of her eyes again, a reflex she always used when she needed to make eye contact for serious conversation. "I needed to get as far away from distractions as possible, so I'm going to the middle of nowhere, to Northeastern in the middle of nowhere North Louisiana, only because out of state tuition is too much." She considered the alternative: party college, same old crews, and the stark possibility that she might end up like her older friends, jobless, aimless and futureless.

"Well, it's obvious we can't stop you," Jeb surrendered. He held his big, oversized hands up. "It's just a shame we'll have to do without our favorite little thief."

"Hey," she shot back, her eyebrows furrowing in weak complaint, "I'm an assassin." She smiled, leaning back and taking a big swig of the root beer. It was creamy, with the kind of malted vanilla flavors that hid beneath the mellow carbonated syrups, "...and a damn good one, at that."

She started to tear up, and Jeb got visibly uncomfortable, shifting his stance awkwardly. "No tears from the cold-blooded assassin, now." That got a small laugh from her. "And you let us know next time you're in town. Two years of straight campaign missions have been great and all, but we'll squeeze you in for a day of excitement and adventure. Don't forget I'm still the king of one-shots."

"That's what she said," Caro offered. She packed up the last of her things, and said goodbye to the small, faithful crew of boys that had been the main source of fun for the majority of her high school days. Those days would have to be put behind her, and she knew that hanging on to the way things were would only make things tougher.

Later that night, she packed all of her books, posters and games up into the first box that would ship out. She figured that as soon as she got a physical address for her new place, these little distractions would be her best salvation from the agonizing torture of being without real friends again. It had taken a lifetime of tries to make these great friends, and yet she only had four years of college to find some kind of counterfeit substitute that would ease the pain of being away from home. The fact that she would be studying engineering was a small consolation. She was sure that geeks of all shapes and sizes would abound on campus, but being surrounded by other people her age who were good at math, interested in engineering, and open to a challenge meant that she would have little problem finding people in her classes who would share her enthusiasm for the game.

No doubt, it would be much harder once she found these comrades in arms to actually talk to one. In her experience, the gamer guys were nearly impossible to talk to. Even worse, once she did talk to them, the kind of guys who were able to have real friendships, much less real relationships, was staggeringly rare. She would have to take the lead. Her father had prepared her for all sorts of situations in gaming, and her mother always tried to give advice on how to talk to boys. Sometimes she wondered how the two of them ever hit it off, given their wildly different perspectives on socialization.

She walked across her half-packed room, past the wall of holes where manga posters once hung, and dug in the box of games. She picked up her guide to being a game master and thumbed through the pages. If she must steer her own social interactions, she mused, perhaps she could learn a thing or two from the Jebs of the world. Perhaps she could lead, and make a few friends through the game that raised her.

THREE

Caro's mother sat across from her in the gas station diner in central Louisiana, grinning broadly. She had just finished her burger and started in on her fries, chattering on about her old college days. "You'll love it, honey. I promise." Far from Caro's father's fine red hair, her mother's black curly locks fell over each shoulder, hinting at her French heritage. Her silk blouse and pearls clashed with the wood paneling of small diner, making her stand out even more than her lack of any kind of Louisiana accent. "You know, when I was back in school–"

"Barbara, just–" the interjection had been unintentional, and beyond her ability to suppress. Caro could already see the look of resignation forming on her mother's face and pangs of guilt settled in. "I'm sorry, I didn't..." she took a bite to compose herself. Calling her mother by her first name was always a terrible idea, and she rarely did it beyond her days of trying to get her mother's attention in the lowest years of high school. Her chicken and white gravy was already cold, and not helping for inspiration. "I'm sure it was wonderful, but it was different for you. I mean, you did the sorority thing, you met Dad." She picked up her tray of mostly uneaten food and headed for the trash can. "You had a whole life there. That's not what I'm looking for. This is just a… a placeholder."

Barbara took a deep breath, cleared her throat and stood, swallowing her protests and shaking the anger away. She put her tray up and walked out the glass door, barely ringing the courtesy bell. Caro followed her out to the car, throwing her own food out as they exited the building, except for her Coke. In the parking lot, her mother spoke softly, "You don't know what God's got in store for you there, honey. You'll see. It's all going to be better than whatever you're imagining now. College is a grand time, I promise."

Caro had a hard time believing that. Her mother sent her to camps the year after her father passed away, always saying the same thing. "Before you know it, you'll be having a grand time," had become her mother's mantra, and perhaps it worked for her. Maybe Caro wasn't forgetful enough. Perhaps if she were only better at forgetting.

Caro's mother's CR-V left first, with Caro's smaller sedan following close behind. The majority of the trip was a single highway that zigzagged through sleepy towns and cleared patches of trees. The highway seemed to creep into each city, deciding only when it got there which was the best way out of town. Often, just after it passed downtown it would make a sharp right, having served its purpose for each settlement. It seemed completely unattached to any one road for long.

The rest of the drive north was quiet. Caro mulled over the coming weeks in a strange new place as country stations faded into pop and then into news radio. She had been so excited just a few months before, but it was harder leaving the old group behind than she had ever let on. She wanted a quiet place, she longed for her spot by her father's grave to talk things through. Her mother told her that everything was going to be alright. That was her job... but Caro couldn't imagine that this new college experience would be anything like the picturesque dream that her mother had often told her about so fondly. The "lifelong friends" that supposedly would stay with you after only four years of classes seemed like a cheap imitation of the friends that had already been there through thick and thin. These friends, Caro imagined, would be much more like the high school friends that were convenient enough when you ran into them four times a day in the halls of school, but faded as quickly as they formed.

Two hours later, they were driving past perfectly manicured lawns into the entrance of Northeastern Louisiana University and pulling up to a short, wide three-story dormitory encased in red brick. A single oak tree in the middle of a circle drive provided the only shade in this collection of dorms, a natural blemish among concrete and brick walls. Caro signed in on the first floor as her mother began pulling wheeled carts from the back of her crossover. When Caro opened the door to her new room, she felt a small burst of hope. Anime scrolls plastered one wall, along with a small collection of manga on a bookshelf in the nearest corner. "Cool."

"Cool?" Her mother seemed surprised. "What is all this?"

"Nothing, Mom." It was something. It wasn't much, but it was at least a good sign. Caro never read the Japanese comic books before, but where there was manga, there was sure to be a gamer.

On the second trip of hauling stuff from the car, Caro walked in to find a tall girl with blonde wavy hair unloading paint brushes into a plastic tote under one of the two small beds. She knelt beside the brown metal frame and upended the rest of the contents of the plastic bookstore bag into the tote. Black charcoal, tubes of oil paints and several pencils spilled into a chaotic pile on top of what seemed to Caro to be a hundred pounds of much of the same. She looked up and smiled big. "New roomie, I take it?"

Caro set a laundry basket of bedding on her dormitory mattress and stepped in to shake her hand. "Yeah, just came up from Baton Rouge." Caro's mom walked in behind them with a box of bathroom items, and Caro nodded her head her mom's way. "My mom drove up with me. Uh, Mom? This is…"

"Genevieve." The blonde girl replied. She smiled, pushing her already high cheekbones up into her eyes, so much that she began to squint. "It's very nice to meet you." Genevieve leaned into a firm handshake with Caro, leaning over the bags and boxes that littered the largely unpacked room.

"I'm Caro."

"Uh, where should I put your shower stuff, Honey?" Barbara circled slowly, pausing at sections of counter space with little obvious organization. Sections of books had packs of ramen noodles mixed in with them. DVDs and books fought for dominance on another section of the counter that was also spattered with video game controllers and a brown leather belt.

Caro took a brief count of the doors. One door, one exit.

"Yeah," Genevieve sighed a small pang of regret. "Communal bathrooms and showers. You'll get used to it." Genevieve walked over to a large locker and opened it to reveal a plastic contraption hanging from the door. "I brought a shower caddy from home years ago. Without much room in here, you learn to hang what doesn't have to take up floor and counter space."

Caro mentally stuffed everything she owned into one of these small rooms when she first decided to move into a dorm. She brought half of her stuff, thinking she would unpack over the fall, bringing more back with her when she returned after Thanksgiving. After looking around at the space available, she began to wonder where she would fit everything she brought.

After the last of the boxes were brought in, Caro's mother let out a heavy sigh. "Well, looks like you girls have everything else covered. I've got a long drive ahead of me."

Caro tried not to think about her mother turning around and leaving. She tried to convince her mother that the trip should be a two-day adventure for them, giving her mother enough time to rest in a local hotel before making the drive back. She longed for a road trip like in the old days, where her mother and father would sprint off to the destination: Tennessee, Colorado, or Florida. Once arriving, they would spend a few days there, then work their way back slowly, meandering like a small brook or a wistful child unwilling to rush back to the real world. Instead, Caro expected her mother to spend an hour tonight going over paperwork at home before going into work bright and early tomorrow. She had gotten a day out of her. She supposed she shouldn't have expected more.

With her mother gone, catalysts for conversation escaped her. She always felt more secure around other girls when her mother was around, like it was okay for her to be excited about science and to talk about advancements in the scientific and political community. With just the two of them in the room, Caro alternated between unpacking and sitting in awkward silence, willing herself to be more social.

"So what's your major?" Genevieve finally asked.

"Electrical Engineering," Caro smiled. "My dad was an electrical engineer. It seemed to make sense, anyway." Genevieve cringed slightly. "Not a fan of engineering, I take it?"

Genevieve shook her head, rolling her eyes exhaustedly. "Nah. I tried. Not really my thing. I like math, and all. I just wasn't ready for it. It's a real different kind of hell."

"Well, don't sugar coat it for me," Caro chuckled.

"Nah. You might be fine. You look smart, like… scientist smart, or something. I'm sure you'll make out okay."

"I hope so." She pulled out her father's old slide rule. She dusted it off when she pulled it out of the attic the week before. She figured if she couldn't take her happy place with her, she would at least have some small piece of him here with her. She put it on her desk by the lamp, stepped back, and decided it was a good place for it. "What about you? All of that paint stuff I saw earlier… you're an art student, I take it?"

"Yeah. I was spending so much time working on stuff that didn't make me happy, I figured it was time for a change." She held up a picture of a group of eight, all gathered around the tree that Caro recognized from the circle driveway. "Tried the engineering thing for a while: chemical, as a matter of fact. That was a long time ago." She showed the picture to Caro. "Most of those people are gone now. I spent long hours on homework that I wasn't all that into. I heard that a studio art degree was hard work, and I'm okay with that. I just figure if I'm going to spend all my waking hours on projects, it should be something I love."

Caro tried to picture it: telling stories, making a living off of doing the one thing that made her happy. She would wake up every morning, needing to tell a story just to pay the bills. She would sell her dream and buy a life with it. She surmised that it would sell pretty cheaply. She would become the starving artist, always having to remind people that at least she was doing what she loved… and she would pay forty thousand dollars in tuition to get there.

"Ugh," she cringed, "you must not like money very much."

Genevieve stood up, half-smiling and eyes starting to shine in the fluorescent lighting of the small room. She walked toward the door. "You haven't been here long, roomie. I'll give you that one for free." She looked her in the eye as the first tear fell. "We've all got dreams. Smart, creative, wonderful kids all over this campus wake up smiling, so confident that all the pain and suffering that they go through to get there is worth it.

"Do yourself a favor and try not to step on anyone else's dreams. Otherwise, you might find that this little campus you ran off to, so far away from home? Well, it's going to get real big and empty."

Caro was fraught. Before anything close to an apology could come out, Genevieve had already walked out leaving her frozen in place. The words that came out of her mouth didn't sound anything like 'wow, you're so brave,' or 'I admire you for how high you seem to prioritize your dreams over the material wealth that society judges others by.' Nope. She felt like a silly little girl. Worse, her first impression on anyone had been hurtful and flippant. Her mother's wooing stories of college memories and friendships had gotten off to a rocky start with the one person that Caro imagined she would be seeing most.

She tried not to think about it too much. Even if she wanted to run out the door and find Genevieve somewhere on campus, she didn't imagine she stood much of a chance of finding her with evening fast approaching and no idea what any other part of the campus looked like. The only person on campus that knew her name was crying because of her. She felt like it must be some kind of record, but even worse, she wondered if this might herald the beginning of a terrible streak for her. She took a seat on her imaginary throne of missteps, bad impressions, and hard feelings. She looked ahead to four years with no friends. She unpacked a few shirts and a pair of jeans before making her bed and calling it an early night.

Genevieve returned sometime shortly after midnight. Caro pretended to be asleep, but Genevieve pulled her chair up next to Caro's bed and sat down a few feet away.

"I've heard it all before, roomie." A faint waft of alcohol hung in the air. "I didn't expect to hear it from someone so new here."

"I'm sorry," Caro began, "I–"

"I'm not done."

I'm such an idiot. I'm sorry I hurt you. I could really use a friend right now. None of these words came out.

"There was this guy in my old engineering class. First day of class, he spills a full-size coffee on the floor in our new lab. Professor tells him the floors haven't been stained yet, and now nothing and I mean nothing is going to keep the floor from forever showing this guy's first mistake in our first class." She laughs to herself. "That guy? That guy that we all thought wasn't going to make it? He got the only A on our first exam, because when the rest of us thought that this college game was going to be just like high school, only with older people, that guy was busting his ass every day to prove that he had what it takes to stay.

"I'm sorry. Hell, I don't even know if I can say 'ass' in front of you. Shit. I'm a little drunk right now. I earned it." Genevieve breathed heavily for a beat. "You earned it, too. I said I was going to give you that one because you were new. I'd like to believe you're like him – you mean well, and you'll do what it takes to make up for those days when you stick your foot in your mouth. There's no clean slate once a hurtful word's been said, I'm not saying that. I think you can make up for it, though. Let's try again tomorrow... whenever you're ready."

"Okay."

Going to college had always sounded like just one step above high school for Caro. Far from it, she felt lost in a maze of buildings, people and nature. Where high schools had large, open fields of grass that students used for parking, the university had expansive networks of sidewalks, trees, gardens and fountains. What she loved most was a fountain that was erected in the middle of eight sidewalks. There, it sat as an epicenter of peace, always on the way to somewhere, if you chose to make it. She found a new hiding place there in the middle of everyone where she could listen to the waters running off stone and burbling in the pool below. The benches that surrounded the Lady of the Mist were a mixture of wrought iron and stained oak, which lent itself equally to the nature around them and the tall buildings.

She spent most of her first afternoons that fall in front of the fountain, working away at homework and trying to stay ahead of some magical curve that no one knew for sure existed. It was a full two weeks before the first tests came, and she felt ready. Math had always been her favorite subject in high school, so she looked forward to the engineering calculus that would be on the tests. She wanted to see how these tests would be. She looked forward to proving herself in the first fires of college. She had been so wrapped up in this pursuit that with the exception of the polite introductions she made to her dorm roommate and the people in her classes, she hadn't shared a connection with anyone by the time she sat down for the first exam.

The room was unusually cold. The air conditioning in the math building was unpredictable at best, and often times felt malicious. Clean chalkboards flanked her at either side, with a whiteboard in front of her with three lines listing only the date, the class number and the test number. There in the classroom, she arranged her calculator and pencils while the front left side of the class studied frantically, hoping to cram some last bit of information in before the tests were passed out, and a third of the back right side of the classroom hadn't showed up yet.

Her math professor walked in, a slight Chinese man with hair that never quite sat on his head fully. He went over the rules of the test in a thick accent, often repeating himself when asked. The rules seemed pretty obvious. No cheating, abide by the university honor code, and no calculators –

That couldn't be right. How could she take a math test without a calculator? Was she even in the right place? She was suddenly unsure. The rest of the class seemed equally perplexed, with the exception of an unshaven older student in the back who looked as if this was not his first attempt. Somehow, that didn't instill any confidence. When the professor looked up from his stack of test papers, he noted the confusion and tried to ease the tension on the students' faces.

"This is nothing to worry about," he insisted with heavy inflection. "Every answer will be simple enough to be solved without calculator. If you must divide or multiply, it should be in even, easily manipulated numbers."

Good, she thought, at least there will be an easy way to know if I'm on the right track. A few minutes later, she was staring into the mouth of madness. Each answer looked wrong, VERY wrong. Many came out to irrational fractions, like sores on a diseased test. It became a writhing zombie form, consuming her confidence and eating away at her weeks of preparation. When the final question came, she couldn't begin to know how to solve it. She drew the best dragon she could, and under its sharp talons, drew a knight reaching for a calculator just out of arm's reach. She finished her drawing before the time was up for the test.

On the way out, several of the students put their heads together to discuss the remains of the bloody battle. Most seemed just as frantic as she. A few offered hints at the correct answer, and a particularly outspoken girl suggested that if they had worked the extra practice problems, they would have had no problem with the exam. "Dr. Hu gave us everything we needed," she offered through cheery brown eyes. She sat down with the few that remained to start pointing at problems in their textbook. Her dark, smooth skin made the white of the pages stand out all the more prominently. Some of the students tried rebutting with simple question numbers, but she simply shook her head as gorgeous dangly earrings clinked against each other.

Caro was feeling too nauseous to join in. She knew this girl, Juneau, well enough to call her by name, but not well enough to show her this anxious, frantic side. She chose to compose herself in her room instead, piled under oversized covers and a stuffed orc that her father gave her when she was 10. It was the oldest thing she owned, and it always brought comfort when too much change got the best of her. She considered tutoring, even though she had always been the tutor in High School. Shouldn't school have prepared her better for this? Shouldn't all of her studying have paid off a little better?

Sometime during the day, her roommate Genevieve came in and started to type on her computer. Soon after she realized that

Caro was sobbing into her white fluffy pillow, Genevieve got back up and headed toward the door.

"I'm sorry," Caro offered.

Genevieve looked at the door for a few seconds, before dropping her hands beside her. "Alright, I give. What's up?" She rubbed the side of worn jeans and raised her eyebrows to inquire for more. She sat on the bed beside Caro as details of the disastrous first exam came spilling out.

"Well of course you didn't ace it," she offered. "How much extra did you do?"

Caro tried to think back. The extra practice problems were untouched, because she always skipped them. The extra problems she was given in high school were always only for the students who felt like they were struggling. When was the last time she felt like she didn't get it before today? She tried to remember what that felt like.

"Sorry to tell you, but A's aren't handed out to the people who do the minimum."

Caro suddenly felt defensive. "How would you know? How long did you stick it out, anyway?"

"Hey," Genevieve shot back, "I was an engineering student for two years. I finished those math classes you hate so much, but by then I knew that it wasn't for me. Maybe you'll learn the same thing."

Genevieve went back to her computer and started working absent-mindedly as she continued to explain. "I learned what I could and could not put up with from school, and I chose to take my beatings in the art studio, where at least I've made something I like by the time I go home at the end of the day."

"I worked two hours a day on homework, though. You don't understand–"

"Then work 8." Genevieve wasn't budging. "How much time do you think art students spend slaving on sketches, canvases and photos? How much time do you think the architecture students spend on their models?" Caro was starting to slouch. Her sobbing turned to self-loathing and self-pity. "Welcome to college. You didn't think this would be easy, did you?"

At that, Caro only shrugged. Easy seemed relative. She never felt like things came easy to her. She always tried to recall the work that she put into everything, and then apply it to every new project. She knew she would have to work hard at this new endeavor, and she felt the weight piling up on her. She desperately wanted an ally that had been through it all before. "Could you teach me?"

Genevieve sat back on the mattress, a delirious giggle erupting from her. "Oh, you don't want my help. I can tell you where to go, though. Have you found the student who knows all the answers yet?"

Caro pictured Juneau working with the students who probably did better than her on the test, and imagined she wouldn't want to go over it all again. "I'll try," she considered, "but I don't want to pester anyone."

"Well, if the brains of the classroom won't help, find an upper classman who can. If anyone can relate to what you're going through, it's those guys."

Caro recalled the guy who looked like he was trying the class again, and then thought better of it. "How can I find them if I'm not in any classes with them?"

"Ask around," Genevieve offered. "Ask your friends." When Caro didn't change her defeated look, Genevieve continued, "You do have friends, right?"

There it was again. That sinking pit in her stomach she avoided so well for the past few weeks. She was lonely, and school and imaginary worlds could only do so much to relieve the twisting knife. She imagined talking to new people. Talking to her roommate had been difficult enough. It had been weeks, and the two were constantly around each other. Still, they barely knew anything about the other. Caro imagined she was much to blame. She successfully shut out every reminder of the real world.

"Genevieve, I don't even know how to–"

Genevieve grabbed her hand, quieting her nervous babbling. She realized she was rambling, and put on her best deer-in-the-headlights look she could muster. "Start by calling me Evie," she offered. "Lucky you," she continued, moving closer to her on the bed in the dorm, "all of your upperclassmen helped me through those math classes that eat your soul."

"Come on. Let's go." Evie got up and headed for the door, grabbing her clutch on the way out. "We'll start with the introductions tonight. They'll be eating soon."

"Ugh. Not the cafeteria. I don't think I could stomach it today."

Evie walked over to where Caro sat on her bed, pulling her up from the mountain of covers and pillows. "Not tonight. You'll soon learn that anyone who has survived long enough here has learned when it's safe to eat at the cafeteria. It's spaghetti and corn night, so we're heading where the veterans eat real food." Evie grabbed one arm and attempted a fireman's carry, pulling Caro up by the shoulders. "We're going to Taco Bell."

Caro guffawed, straining against being picked up but finally relenting. "Fine! Fine!" She brushed the wrinkles out of her clothes as best as she could. "You win this time. I'll socialize."

Taco Bell was packed with people Caro never saw on campus, but they all seemed just about the right age. Every corner contained a different group, too. In one booth in the corner, a group of boys sat working on three laptops, all attached to a robot that sounded as if they were trying to get it to whistle the Star Wars theme song. There were three guys and a girl sitting at a booth closest to the food, going over lecture notes and with a pile of index cards in the middle. Still in line, three Indian guys waited for their food while comparing what Caro assumed were ringtones, laughing and taking turns.

"Not a lot of girls here, are there?"

Evie pulled Caro in by the hand, making her way toward the laptop boys. "Of course not, but you wanted to meet the guys that could help, right?" The boys looked up at Evie's tall, stacked frame as she came closer. A slight blond boy raised a hand in salute to receive a high five from her. His pin-striped trilby crowned long blond hair that went past his shoulders.

Evie collected the high five and pulled Caro from behind her. The two couldn't have been more different: Caro was smaller, with a wispy frame that hid beneath oversized t-shirts and skinny jeans.

She stood with one hip slightly farther out than the other, as if leaning against a wall or post, while Evie stood tall, enjoying every inch of her height.

Evie held Caro by the shoulders, "Boys, this is Caro. Play nice, and this one might stick around." She pulled Caro in close to make introductions around the table. "Wil is your math guy. He'll help you through any of your problems." She gestured toward the trilby. "He was a Mathlete in his home town, and hasn't stopped since. I think he's crazy, because he switched from engineering to a pure math degree. He says he didn't like the practical stuff." Wil gave a half wave, pulling a limp left forearm from his right shoulder to the crown of his head.

"This is Aidan." Evie motioned to a tall boy in the middle of the pack, typing furiously into a laptop. He leaned in closer to the screen, examining his code before pushing enter and looking up with a grin. The robot let out a sharp wolf whistle of approval. "He's a bit of a heathen, but if you don't mind the creepy jokes, he's mostly harmless." Aidan raised his eyebrows and smiled a little. This one appeared almost social.

"Finally," Evie waved a hand to Chad, "meet Chad." Chad jumped up from his seat at the far end of the table with a flourish and giving a weak 'Enchanté'. "NO, Chad. Down." Evie verbally whipped him into submission and then pointed back to his seat, waiting for a confirmation he'd understood. He looked back at Evie, then down to his spot on the bench. "SIT."

Evie pulled Caro back, "I'm sorry about him. This is the only warning I can give. Chad is a little…" she struggled with her words, "girl crazy. Except, he's never actually been with a girl."

"I can hear you," Chad called from his seat at the table, earning a nudge from Aidan.

"So…?" Caro questioned.

"So, I give him a month. He'll ask you out, and probably act like it's the end of the world if you refuse."

It seemed strange. No doubt, Evie knew her boys better than Caro did, but the sharp way that she spoke with him made Caro wonder if she ever took the time to actually get to know him, or if she just wrote him off like so many people wrote off Caro, as the misunderstood anti-social girl who would never understand boys. She understood boys well enough, until it came down to the one in a million that she crushed on. For some reason, it always changed the rules. Caro hated that.

After the girls picked up their food, they pulled chairs around the corner booth to talk business. The boys seemed as interested in Caro's professors, classes and assignments as they were about her interests. Each one had their own opinions about the professors, and how best to prepare for the exams.

"Hu always uses the extra practice questions," Aidan offered, "He'll change the numbers, but the structure is the same." It made sense. Perhaps these boys could save the day after all.

"Just wait until Robertson," Wil offered. The other boys groaned in unison.

When no further information seemed forthcoming, Caro bit. "What's wrong with Robertson?"

Chad chimed in. "Robertson is a total Monte Cook. Interesting word problems, impossible solutions."

"Monte Cook, like the game designer?" Caro couldn't believe it. "Like," for emphasis, "THE game designer?"

"Yeah," Chad laughed. "Good luck getting out of that one alive. You know Monte Cook?"

"Of course!" Caro bubbled over, "He's what got me interested in becoming a dungeon master!"

"– Dungeon mistress," Aidan interjected, holding a hand up like a point of order.

"Bad dog," Evie shot back, smacking the back of his hand. "Keep it clean in front of the new blood."

"Mistresses live at the whim of their masters," Caro taunted back. "I am a dungeon master. Cross me, little man," she put on her best sinister voice, "and see what becomes of your fate."

Evie's eyes rolled at the jaws agape on the other side of the table. "You are SO hired. Would you consider joining the table?"

"You game?" Caro pictured her Norwegian art student sitting at a table and rolling dice, crying triumphant at the fall of the orcish horde. It wasn't fitting.

"You really have no idea. That's okay." Evie tried to fill her in over supper while the boys tossed questions at her to see what she knew of role playing games. Her father's obsession with all things gaming prepared her better than anyone else, and she was glad for it. Her hobby that made her feel like an outsider among most of the people in high school gave her a back door into a close-knit group of friends, and she hoped to make the most of it.

It didn't take long to exhaust the boys' knowledge of games. She tried to push them further, asking about fantasy lands from canon books, and pushing hypothetical conversations of deities in game settings. "They really don't play," Evie told her. "I'm trying to get them started, but it's not easy with school schedules. Not to mention, none of us have any idea where to start."

Caro bubbled over on the inside, and her enthusiasm came gushing out when she pulled a sketchbook from her messenger bag. She agreed in some ways. 'Where to start' was indeed an excellent question, but she had plenty of options. She dropped the sketchbook onto the table, flattening the pages of a map with smatterings of forests and mountain ranges. "Why not start in Rillis?"

The boys and Evie pored over the notebook, with detailed geographical, political and sociological maps. Character sketches followed every major town, with the big players in each area having full biographies. Each dungeon square in her green engineering paper was filled with notes, shading and flavor, bringing the world to life in a brief glimpse. When Caro felt like the four had seen enough, she grabbed it back. "What's the fun in discovering a world you've already read through?"

Wil stood from his seat, sitting back down with his foot between his opposite leg and the bench to get a better look at the book. "I've never seen anything like it," he admitted. "Caro, if you can give me an hour a day, I'll get you through math."

Caro considered her scholarship and the stacks of ramen in her dorm room, "I couldn't pay," she began.

"No need. You give us one night a week of a real game, and that's all the reward I need."

FoUR

The cave that sat slightly below ground level in the dorms used to be a frequent go-to for movie nights and other activities, but since the first week of school it hadn't seen much use. Evie helped Caro rearrange the couches and chairs around a single long table, making room for Caro's first game night as Game Master. She loved the worlds she built, knew every nook and cranny and all of the characters by name and deed. She still had no idea what she was in for. No one ever interacted with these people. They were almost sacred to her. She hoped they wouldn't give Markus a hard time. He'd already been through so much.

"You'll be fine," Evie assured her.

"What if they don't want to do what I need them to do?"

Evie laughed and shook her head. "So what if they don't? The more you let them have fun, the more fun you'll have. Trust me."

By the time the boys arrived, snacks were laid out and Caro had set up a corner for herself where she could put all of her notes, away from prying eyes. Wil showed up in his classic trilby, along with an anime shirt of some show Caro had never heard of. Its blacks and pinks and whites came together in a chaotic mess on his chest. No doubt, the show was one of many that Caro didn't get. More and more, her friends tried to tell her about these shows, but they all seemed to have less storyline and more randomness in an attempt to hold the modern gamer's dwindling attention span.

Aidan came in wearing a worn red shirt with a panda on the front. Caro hadn't gathered that Aidan held any affection for panda bears. She wondered if there was anything in his closet that he really liked. Guys were weird like that. They'd wear anything, even if it meant nothing to them. Chad followed closely behind, with a huge backpack weighing him down. When he sat at the table, he began pulling out books, miniatures, dice, a dice tower, and even a fancy pencil holder case with a twenty-sided die etched into it. Caro quickly ascertained the veteran of the group.

Everyone seemed to have a character ready but Wil, who sat quietly taking in the scene. He scratched his head nervously when people started talking, but every time he opened his mouth, the giddy conversation seemed to drown him out.

"What's up?" Caro waved at him, pulling him out of his bubble of hesitation.

"I just… I have no idea what I'm doing. I've got this sheet in front of me. I think I'm…" he looked for a solid two minutes at the page, eyes scanning from box to box trying to decipher a grand riddle, "a… monk?"

Aidan twirled a pencil on his fingers, looking over to Wil. "We need a monk. You can resist most magical effects, you get decent attacks, and you're already quiet anyway. It was a good fit."

Wil didn't seem so sure. Caro picked up the character sheet reading it. "You made this, Aidan?" Aidan nodded.

Wil shrugged. "I've never played before. I told him to make something good."

"Hardly sounds like it matters to you," Caro suggested, "but who do you want to be?" When Wil didn't suggest anything, she continued. "Close your eyes."

A dirt road trailed off before and after him, and he was alone. His anime shirt twisted and morphed into mush. His form lost all definition, and he floated toward the trees.

"You like heights? Are you a Tarzan kind of guy, or more like Tolkien's elves?"

He wrapped a slender arm around the trunk of the tree, and golden skin glowed against the bark. Leaves fell from above him, catching in his long dark hair. Already, his high cheekbones started to become more sharply defined as fine leather brocade vest wrapped him securely.

"Here's where your character really comes to life," Caro spoke quietly and evenly. "There's one thing that your character does that's awesome. It's his purpose. It's the reason why you came here."

Elvish hands closed around a deep black ivory. The shaft grew until it was almost two thirds of his height.

"Picture him at his best, doing the one thing that makes your character yours."

A fine spider silk thread wrapped the top and bottom of the black ivory bow, and Wil drew back an obsidian arrow, drawing a bead off in the distance. Wind whipped his hair behind him as he made out an orc's head five hundred feet in the distance. Aidan stood on the ground, leaning against his staff and watched dubiously.

"You look ridiculous. What are you?"

"I am the Night Stalker," Wil loosed his arrow well above the target. It flew for what felt like thirty seconds, angling down with the wind and landing squarely in the eye of the orc in the distance.

"There's no such thing as a night stalker," Aidan chuckled. "You're an archer."

Caro walked along the tree tops, floating in glowing alabaster robes. "Night Stalker. He's right, you know. There has never been one before, but you're so much more than an archer." Wil climbed down from the tree to join Aidan just as Evie's white-haired rogue walked up. "Your character is yours alone. I like it. You're not pouring yourself into a cookie-cutter mold and saying, 'Well, I guess I have to be an archer, because that's the rules.' Not a bad first game."

Chad's rippling ball of muscles joined in, gleaming in his plate armor, spinning a maul in one hand like Charlie Chaplin's cane. He looked the archer up and down, sneering in disdain. "Seems awfully squishy. Better be extra careful with that one."

"Why?" Wil looked around him. "What happens if my character dies?"

"That's it." Evie said. "Game over."

Caro's head picked up. "Game over? Is that really how you see it?" They all shrugged in agreement.

She carried them down the path to a fork, where deep woods lay to the left and a mountainous cavern lay to the right. "If these woods burn down, the trees are gone, but the land still has a story to tell," she offered. "If there is a cave-in, everything in the mountain is trapped, but its story goes on, isolated from the rest of the world until the next adventurer finds his way inside."

Aidan's wizard glanced at the hourglass on his wrist. "Well, let's get moving. Who do we have to see first?"

Aging stone outer walls wrapped around the party. Muddied guards eyed them suspiciously as a grizzled captain looked the party over with golden spectacles. They stood just inside the rim of a great walled city, where beggars, merchants and farmers filed in to make their meager livings. The party seemed like outsiders, wearing the hardy adventuring garb that largely withstood the regular wear and tear that turned the commoner's clothing into tatters, but didn't shine with gaudy affluence of the merchants' gilded fabrics.

"This lot won't make it far inside the gates if they're not careful." The captain nudged his guards before walking among the party. "There are cutpurses who will take what's not nailed down if you aren't careful," he said, eyeing the rogue with a smirk. "I imagine the wizard would like to speak to Serena the Sage if he's come looking for answers of a magical nature. The elf can't be here seeking passage to the High Elven Tribe to the north. Not unless he plans on putting out the ashes of the burned lands that used to be the elven tribe." He moved back to Evie's rogue, eyeing a pendant around her neck. "I imagine you might seek the original owner of that item, seeing as how you'd have to be a shadow priest to claim rightful ownership of this." Finally, he stood before the brute. "I can't imagine this one here coming into town to do anything but pick a fight. Best be sure I'll *have my eye on you. Let's not cause too much trouble, eh?"*

The captain stood back from the doors, and the main brick road to the city opened out before them. Aidan pushed ahead, making his way to the first intersection which was filled with food carts, an empty gallows and a well with peasants lined up to fill their jugs with water. The wizard circled briefly, taking in the crossroads with suspicion.

"I don't get it."

Muddy streets turned to concrete flooring. The signposts surrounding the crossroads turned to the familiar couches that filled the dorm's common area seemingly without rhyme or reason. The small group found themselves back at the gaming table, munching on cheese balls while half of them managed the logistics of cups, cokes and ice.

"What do you mean?" Caro was baffled. "You can do whatever you want," At her end of the table, her notebook was already laid out to three possibilities behind her cardboard screen as Aidan shook his head in confusion.

"No. It doesn't work like that." He looked around at the motley crew that played with dice and miniatures. "What are the odds everyone will want to go in the same direction? What if we never decide to do anything, and we just spend the entire day wandering through the town picking fights and missing out on the adventure?"

Caro struggled to try to find a down side.

"We'll never make it to second level at this pace." Aidan shuffled his papers together, and then propped his head up with his hands, elbows on the table.

"Does that matter?" Caro questioned the group. She tried to remember the difference between the games she sat down to play with her father compared to the games she played with her old group. When both still seemed like good memories, she tried to remember anyone in either group not having a good time, and the wild tangents that her random friends often brought on themselves.

Between the five of them, they all came to a general agreement that the party would have to get some work done, but by the time the night's festivities came to a close, they had only decided on a general direction to go first thing next week.

Everyone was packing up to leave when Chad came over to the other side of the table. "Thanks for doing this." He looked down at his shoes, shifting his weight between his feet.

Caro brushed off the words, "It's no big deal, really. How else am I supposed to feel normal if I can't play?" Truth be told, she wasn't feeling totally normal, but having a group again relaxed her, and she felt like she at least had an outlet that made the hectic pace of classes a little better. A twist in her gut reminded her just how far she was from the comfortable life of a few short months ago. Normally, she would be leaving the game and heading to see Chris after work. They'd fall asleep in front of a bad movie and she'd wake up fully recharged. Between the two, they had always been good for setting the world back just the way she liked it, surrounded by people that knew and loved her. These people barely knew her, though.

Chad gave a little laugh under his breath. "Well, if you ever want to go off campus, maybe grab something to eat... I'd be happy to join you. Just let me know."

"Thanks, Chad. I pretty much just eat in the dorm. I keep a pretty strict budget that doesn't leave a whole lot of room for real food, so I'll be in the cafeteria most days."

"Well, I'm just offering." Chad held up his left hand, offering to shake. When Caro reached in with her right hand, the backs of their hands touched awkwardly. He tried to switch hands at the same time as she did, with much the same effect. He shrugged, held out both hands and reached in for a hug. Caro laughed, nodding. She reached in, hugging him gently and gave two friendly pats on the back. She started to pull back, and there was that weird pull when he didn't realize the hug was over. Chad went back to looking at his shoes while Caro eyed him quizzically.

From Evie's spot across the table, she looked up and saw the scene unfolding. She walked closer to Chad, grabbing him by his collar. "Come on back, Romeo." Chad started to blush as Evie turned back apologetically. "What did I tell ya? He's a charmer."

The room cleared as one by one the game pieces were put up and Evie, Aidan and Chad walked out together into the night air. With the rest of the table cleared, math books and notes quickly replaced the maps and character sheets as Caro and Wil sat in front of her homework working through the extra problem set. Wil pointed at another problem, working her through the steps.

"Okay, when it looks like this, take the derivative of both sides, take the bottom part, bring it over to the other side, multiply out and combine. Got it?" The blank look on her face told him that she didn't in fact, have it. He sighed. "14."

"What?"

"I know I said I wouldn't just give you the answers, but this one gets weird. The answer is 14. Do you want to move on to the next one?"

Her mind shifted from math problems to Chad problems. Both seemed equally perturbing, but one was somehow more pressing. "Is Chad going to ask me out?"

Wil smiled. "Math is perfect, people are not. I am, however, more sure that Chad will ask you out than I am sure that the answer to this question is 14."

"Why's he so weird?" Caro dealt with lots of socially awkward boys in gaming. She always felt like she had a target on her because of her love for magic and all things medieval fantasy. Chad was different, and not in her kind of way.

"Do you remember how weird it was in middle school, trying to learn how to talk to people, figuring out what's going on with your body, and still never knowing what a real relationship was supposed to be like?"

"Faintly. I try to forget."

"Well, that's Chad, except everyone else he tries to talk to has already been through it." Caro rolled her eyes at the thought. It couldn't be easy, but she couldn't imagine who would try to break through his insecurities, inexperience and show him how the rest of the world interacts. "He's not a bad guy, but he's making up a lot of ground. We put up with him, and try to steer him away from the bad ones."

Caro took a deep breath, and then powered through the rest of the problems with Wil. She could no sooner grasp the ideas he was trying to teach her than she could teach Chad how to listen to a girl, and hear what she was trying to tell him.

The next day in class, she was feeling the same mixture of lost emotion while the teacher worked through a problem on the board. She looked around, trying to see who was ahead of the curve, who she could ask for help. Juneau seemed to barely pay attention. She was working away at the example problem in her notebook, undoubtedly a few steps ahead of the professor. From the faces she could read in the class, the rest seemed as lost as she was.

"Any questions?" The professor finally turned around when the board was full, and soaked in the silence. He turned the corners of his mouth down in a 'Not bad' as he turned back, eraser in hand, to move on to the next subject. Involuntarily, Caro's hand shot up in the air.

"I don't get it," she said, still wondering how that could be of any help. The professor cocked his head to the side, waiting for more, but nothing came out. He turned to the board, working through the steps in his head as the eraser pointed at each piece of the problem. When he felt satisfied he had covered the problem sufficiently, he turned back to her but she was already looking down at her paper again.

"Please, Miss…" he prodded.

"Uh, Caro. I'm trying to follow, but I still don't get it." The rest of the class started to stare, and she could feel her ears getting hot. She looked back down at her paper, which looked exactly like the board. She wondered if she could work it out on her own after class.

Slowly, the silence spread until the rest of the class realized that the time was nearly up. They began to pack their bags, eager to leave the mess of chalk, symbols and equations behind. Taking their cue, the professor gave in, "I will see you all Wednesday. I will have your tests graded by then." The bustle of shuffling desks and papers was deafening, but still Caro didn't move. She knew she was missing something basic, like it was staring at her but she just sat mortified instead.

Most of the class was gone by the time the professor made his way to Caro's desk. He looked at her notes, satisfied that she caught everything on the board. "Miss Caro, I can help you," he insisted. "I can't, however, if you don't ask."

Her mouth opened, but words dripped out as if from a leaky faucet. "I... don't know where to begin. I just don't get it."

The Chinese professor smiled. "This is your first semester here, right?" She nodded. "I think it is time to teach you something that will help you pass every class you attend at this institution." His heavy accent was strained on the S's, but he worked hard to get his point across, and she was rapt.

"Problem solving? I get it, I mean. Math helps you learn to solve problems–"

"No, Miss Caro. Do you have a minute?" She did. "It is time for you to learn how to ask a question."

She sighed deeply. Now he was just patronizing her. He held his hands up to calm her.

"Close your eyes. Now, what's the first step? Can you see it?"

"Nothing," she shook her head.

"Open your eyes." Dr. Hu was standing in front of the example problem, with only the numerator of the chain rule of division showing. "Do you see it now?"

"I'm looking at it, but–"

"You may look all you like, Miss Caro, but do the symbols make sense?"

She read through the top line, with squiggly lines making a mess of the letters. On one side of the board, messy fractions muddled the process of derivatives. On the other side, apostrophes jumbled with letters until nothing made any sense. In disgust, she shook her head-

"There." The professor wasn't even looking at the board. "What were you looking at when you shook your head?"

She looked again. Apostrophes taunted her from the board. Language rules stopped making sense when she was supposed to do math with them. She had no idea where all the math operators that she knew so well had gone. Instead, she just saw letters thrown together.

The professor waved his hands in front of her, drawing her vision away from the mess of notation. "Low-dee-high-high-dee-low, low-low." A faint flicker of recognition crossed her face. She'd heard Wil say it before, but it was usually prefaced with his shortcuts, and spilling the answer in front of her and leaving her to pick up the pieces of a segmented understanding of the problem.

"The 'dee' is the derivative." He laid out three examples of writing derivatives in front of her, showing her what each meant, and how they used each in their class notes from the previous days.

He worked the steps aloud with her, and she still balked every time he told her that 'dee' was the same thing as an apostrophe. She would have to take him at his word for that.

Every time she got frustrated, he broke apart that portion of the problem to see where her difficulty started. Tears of frustration squeezed out over the next twenty minutes, but no one else was there to see them. Professor Hu didn't seem to notice them either. He only saw when she scrunched her face at a phrase or variable. By the time she left, she could have walked the rest of the class through the lesson, but she couldn't shake the nagging feeling that she'd taken up too much of his time, that she somehow pestered him until he gave up his knowledge begrudgingly.

"I know you can't do this every day," she admitted as she was walking out of the classroom.

"You would be amazed, Miss Caro. My door is always open, and yet the office is usually empty." He offered a gentle smile, one filled with patience and understanding. "The next time you need to ask a question, Miss Caro, seek the origin of your confusion, and if anything else comes up, please don't hesitate to see me during those office hours.

Walking out of the classroom, a wave of relief washed over her. She might just get the hang of this school thing after all.

FIVE

From the blanket of darkness, a dim pile of seared flesh and gold littered the stone floor. The ambush of black trolls nearly did her in, but Evie's rogue would not be beaten to the dividing of the loot. Skittering closer, the caped white-haired gnome cut away at the money pouches and began separating the weapons. "Couple of daggers... a small scimitar... a – hey Kelse, there's a wand in here!" She flipped her long hair behind her, and with her free hand, tied it into a short ponytail. Her pointy ears were one of the few things that reminded the party that she wasn't a child, and she did her best to show her age when they split the spoils of each new conquest.

Kelse moved closer, swishing his crimson robes on the moldy stone floors. The smell of troll blood mixed with fungus and brimstone. It smelled like money. It always smelled like money to Aidan's caster. He took the wand in hands so small, they were almost the same size as the gnome's. He ran his fingers across the gilded glyphs before nodding, "A strength charm. It's no surprise why they were such a tough fight. This might come in handy later." He slipped the wand up his sleeve, and looked to the corner of the room at a figure in the darkness. "How are we doing on time?"

The elven Night Stalker, Alain, called back. "We'll make good time, as long as our brute doesn't cause any more unnecessary distractions." The great giant sulked off on hearing this, dragging his feet through the echoing dungeon caverns as he went. "If our intelligence was right," Alain continued, "we're out of distractions anyway." He moved closer to the gnome and the wizard, pulling a vellum scroll from his belt pouch.

The fine writing on the scroll gave merit to his assertion. Whoever commissioned the scroll had paid well. The center of the map, just one room from where they were standing, indicated the lair of a dragon, promising wealth to the brave adventurers that could slay it. "If I'm right," Alain insisted, "the dragon will still be young, which means if we work together—"

Kachoom! The door slammed shut. From behind it, they could hear the angry roars of the dragon. No one had to count to see who was missing. Only one member could be stupid enough to try to do it on their own.

"Damnit, Grul!" Alain cursed and kicked at the door, but no one on this side of the great stone entrance could do anything to budge it.

They heard the muffled voice of the brute, the best muscle that their money could buy, yell back, "This, I must do for GLORY."

Keelie the rogue poured money in the middle of the three remaining adventurers. "We're going to need a new brute." She started counting gold and mentally going through the available hired help in the nearby city.

A distinctly separate clink came from a gem tossed into the pile of gold by Kelse. "Best ruby I've got says he can do it. You underestimate the man who got us here safely."

Grul squared off against the green dragon. Its scales bristled as it *paced the horde of gold it amassed in its short life. Alain was right. At just over 7 feet, this monster was smaller than the great beasts that scorched their lands and claimed villages, but it was still a threat to be quelled. Grul slid forward, brandishing his great claymore and shouting at it, hoping to catch it off guard.*

It roared back and stood clumsily on its hind legs, a full foot taller than him, and easily 200 pounds heavier. They paced around each other, sizing each other up. Grul pulled a rock the size of his fist from his belt pouch, throwing it at the green devil. Five feet from his hands, the rock turned the size of a boulder, crashing into the dragon. He rushed toward it as it hissed back "You will pay for that, human."

They rushed into each other, a chaotic mess of claws and blade. The dragon tore into Grul's shoulder with a ferocious bite, and Grul grappled him to the ground, pounding away as best he could with his oversized sword. Keelie, Kelse and Alain worked away at the door, trying to unjam what the great barbarian attempted to seal. Another boulder stood just on the other side of the door, defying their efforts.

Both man and dragon began to slow, resorting back to pacing thirty minutes later. Grul bled profusely from his shoulder, and the dragon limped around in a circle. With the last ounce of strength he had, Grul charged forward, swinging wildly with the claymore. The dragon jumped to avoid it, but zigged when it should have zagged. The blade cut deep under its forelegs, pushing deep into its abdomen. With a deathly hiss, it breathed its last breath as Alain, Kelse and Keelie finally managed to push the door open.

"What in the 7 hells, barbarian?" Alain moved closer to inspect

his wounds while the others stood dumbfounded at the carnage. "How's glory feel, Sponge?"

"I am more than just a sponge," Grul called back solemnly, "and I expect I have proved that today... to all of you." Sawing with the mighty claymore, he severed the head of the dragon, rolling it at the feet of the nonplussed and irritated trio.

The walls melted around Grul as his barbarian guise shifted to Chad's black and white shirt with a binary joke about 10 kinds of people. "What are you looking at me like that for?" Caro looked up from her notes at her reckless barbarian. Chad's Grul nearly offed himself in some sort of play for party leadership, and now he looked expectantly at her for some kind of reward. She rolled a purple twenty-sided die at him. It bounced off the maps, the paper, and up against his red solo cup of Mountain Dew. The die came up 1.

"See that?" Caro pleaded, "My crappy rolls are the only reason why you lived. You really think your 5th level character has what it takes to take on any dragon on his own, young adult or not?" She bemoaned her own bad luck, knowing that it probably made him more confident than he needed to be. "Besides, that was crazy going in there alone. What do you think you really proved?"

"I just..." Chad wrung his hands until his knuckles whitened, "I just wanted to prove I was more than a sponge. I can dish out damage, too. I can lead the charge." His cheeks flushed and he shuffled his papers, pulling them into his lap. "I wanted to prove it to you–" he mumbled into his paperwork. He stood up and started packing his character sheet and dice into his backpack. Everyone at the table shifted uncomfortably. Caro looked to Evie, her only estrogen accomplice in the room. Evie seemed shocked, looking at Caro expectantly, a cryptic smile spreading across her face. When Chad left the room, Evie started to laugh.

"What's so funny? And what's up with him, anyway?" Caro tried to play back the last ten minutes to see if she had said anything wrong. She still couldn't wrap her head around someone breaking away from the group to take on a challenge alone. If he wanted to do it by himself, why would he play a tabletop game with the rest of them?

"Oh my god, Caro. You don't get it, do you?" Evie shook her head, smiling. "You should talk to him." The three that remained as Caro followed Chad outside spread out on the sofas in the lounge. The deep blue sofas, the large screen TV and the stone bare floors that placed the student lounge just below ground level had been affectionately called a cave by the rest of the students, but once they started their fantasy role playing, they had taken to calling it their Cave of Wonders.

Outside, the fall leaves began to turn. The yellows and oranges of Louisiana fall began to match the lighter bricks of the dorms on campus, making it look like the buildings were planned for this season. Chad muttered to himself beneath an oak tree, ashes falling from his cigarette onto his binary t-shirt. When she made it beneath the canopy of the tree, mere steps from where he was smoking, she called his name when he still hadn't turned to her.

"Do you want to tell me what's going on?"

"It's stupid. Don't worry about it."

At least he was talking. She tried to make him look her in the eye, but he turned his head away. She side stepped to get in front of him, her brown eyes meeting his. She would need a better answer than that. Everyone else seemed to know the answer but her. He stuttered, "Wh – what difference does it make? I thought you w- would notice me if I could take on the dragon, bu-but…" His voice trailed off.

"Notice you? Is this because Aidan calls you Sponge? Geez, Chad. You're a vital member of the team, and you do good things." She sighed, "Sit down." From under the tree, she tried to get more out of him, but he still would only speak vaguely. Finally, she decided she would have to push until he came out with it. "What's really going on here?"

It was like pulling teeth, or herding cats. Her father used to tell her that getting some boys to talk about their feelings was like trying to nail Jell-O to a tree. She assumed that those days were over after leaving for college, but currently she felt seriously mistaken. She figured she would walk him through it. "I think I know what's going on. Say it with me. Same time, so you don't have to feel weird." Putting himself out there must have been hard enough, she decided. "You… like…"

"I LIKE YOU, alright? Geez. I've liked you since the day we met."

"Chad, that was two weeks ago."

"I know, but when I feel like this, I just can't let this feeling go unspoken, you know?" Chad breathed a sigh of relief, looking her in the eyes softly, so softly.

Oh, no. Caro started running through scenarios in her head, where she didn't have to break his heart, her role playing group could keep the tank, and he would still know that she didn't share his affections. Nothing came to mind. "Chad, I... I," now she was stuttering, shaking her head nervously waiting for him to make the connection on his own.

"Nobody ever likes me." He turned, throwing a half-empty pack of cigarettes on the ground and stomping away.

Caro imagined a school boy pulling his basketball off the court when he missed the shot. I'm taking my ball and going home. "That's it, huh?" Chad turned around, puzzled. "Chad, how many rejections have you gotten in your life?" Her voice was flat and unapologetic. When he only shrugged, she decided to push a little harder. She wouldn't break him, but she wasn't going to baby him, either. "You think it's easy for me? I've put myself out there dozens of times. Most of the time, nothing comes of it because they're taken or not interested or gay. It doesn't mean I stop trying."

"Well, I'm none of those things," Chad offered.

"No. Nooo. No." Three inflections. Maybe that will drive the point home for good. "It's not going to happen. Ever. And that should be okay with you, because how else will you learn about girls if you can't accept 'being friends' as a viable answer?"

Chad's shoulders relaxed, and he smirked, indifferent. She supposed that would have to do for now. She held his hand, and suggested, "When you're ready again, next time you decide to talk to a girl about your feelings, promise me you won't freak out about it?" He smiled a little. She sincerely hoped he didn't think she was joking. "I'll tell you what," she turned back to the dorm behind them and saw the other three players congregating at the door, "you let me know when you're ready to have that talk with the special girl, and I'll tell you what to say."

"I'd like that," Chad said softly. "I suppose we need to divide up the loot before the thief takes it all," he stood up to move back to the dorm.

"Oh, I'll make sure she saves you something." She wasn't losing him after all, and if it killed her, she just might teach him how to be a civilized gentleman.

From the clearing in the middle of the dorm rooms, Caro could see Aidan leaning over the rail as the pair made their way back. "Kiss him!" he cooed as they neared.

Her eyes said 'Don't start,' but she figured that would only make things worse. She would settle for a simple observation. "You're an asshole, did you know that?" She slapped him on the shoulder as she made her way behind them back into the dorm. He did his best to appear innocent, holding his hands up in surrender to Evie. Evie smacked him once, too, for good measure before they all went back into the game room.

SIX

The engineering classrooms were a different animal from the other classes that Caro spent much of her time in. History, like every class in high school, was full of desks where the history lovers flocked to the front row and the carefree stayed out back. Engineering classrooms were divided into two types of sections. The middle row had tables with comfortable armchairs on wheels. A plug centered itself at each table, easily enough to accommodate four people to a table, and one laptop to a person. The far walls held all kinds of tools, from a drill press to soldering irons to riveting guns and press brakes. Conceivably, she was told, everything that they needed to make for their engineering basic assignments could be done inside the classroom.

The first day, she naturally gravitated toward the only other girl in the room, the tall dark-skinned Juneau who became the star player of the calculus class. A short and stout blond boy sat with them, and for the first week she hoped that he was looking for a group equally motivated to make something happen in this, their first attempt at big kid school. It didn't take long to add up the days he didn't make it, and then rely on his regular attempts to copy homework and hit on the two girls. The fourth was an older man, quiet, with a full beard that seemed to obscure his emotions. He was difficult to read, but always weighed his words carefully. The few days that they had to join heads on serious projects, the older student Patrick never failed to provide the lion's share of input.

When midterms passed, and just as Caro was starting to feel as if she might stay afloat, the engineering professor Dr. Dietrich dropped the bomb. When they walked into class, the scruffy six-foot German had a large board with blanks drawn across it. From under his tweed jacket with elbow patches, he puffed his chest in pride at the scampering students taking in the meaning of what he wrote on the board. In the top right corner, he had a space marked off with only words written out in large upper case: GROUP ASSIGNMENTS.

"Well, kiddos," Dietrich smiled, "this is the day you find out what the real meaning of teamwork is."

As it turns out, whoever sat at the table with Caro would be her partner for the rest of the quarter. She hoped beyond measure that her short little blond boy would decide to sleep in. She thought it might be cold enough for him to bite at the thought. Five minutes after class started, just before Professor Dietrich assigned their table, he waltzed in with a large Styrofoam cup and a pencil. That's it.

"And, table 4. Ah, Mr. Lars. I see you have decided to grace us with your presence."

"What?"

And with barely a word, Caro felt her hopes sink into the cold tile floor. Patrick would be a huge help. Juneau, she already knew was a genius. Perhaps they could pull it off even with the dead weight, but she groaned at the inescapable excuse tying her to this useless number four.

The rest of the class was spent brainstorming. Everyone would suggest an idea for a product that would make life easier, and solve a problem. With the limited experience she had so far with her programmable board, she tried to stick to things that she thought could be done. That didn't include much.

After the fourth suggestion for a doggy door that kept other dogs out, that monitored how much time the dog was outside, one particularly sadistic boy in the back suggested a doggy door that was connected to an RFID reader and a guillotine. He suggested that if a strange dog tried to come in, the Doggy Decapitator could get rid of it.

"Let's just assume that all doggy doors are out," Dietrich offered. "It's been done once, twice, sometimes three times every semester. I promise, whatever you think you can make the doggy door do, it's been done before.

By the end of the class, there were twenty suggestions, and they all sounded too boring or too complicated to pull off properly. Caro exchanged numbers with the rest of her table, and asked if anyone wanted to meet up over coffee or pancakes to consider more interesting alternatives. Patrick and Lars shrugged off the idea. She made eye contact with Juneau, who smiled sideways.

"Fine by me, but if you want to brainstorm tonight, you'll have to follow me to Sundown." She began packing her laptop and books away. "It's blues night, and there's nothing else in this town worth staying up late for."

Caro didn't hear much after blues. It was a staple of the fairs and festivals of southern Louisiana. Old cover bands might not have time to learn all the latest hits, but each of them knew pitch perfect covers of Purple Rain, Crossroads, and Texas Flood. If Sundown was near as good as this, she figured it would be just as good a place as any to shuffle off the school brains where all answers were given, and move on to new ideas.

She met up with Juneau later that day, just as the evening trains began to make their way through the sleepy college town. A half brick and half wrought-iron fence separated the outdoor bar from the sidewalk, and she could hear sounds of electric guitar and bass flowing from the stage at the back of the building. Juneau was at a table nearest the street, sipping on a goblet of amber beer and smoking a cigarette. She looked at home here, so far away from the awkward engineering students, and away from the school refreshments of sodas, lattes and water bottles.

Caro stepped in, laying her messenger bag at her feet and trying to angle herself so she could see the sunset over the bars and still get a good view of the band. She soon found she would have to decide, and opted for the band. She loved the tangle of cords and instruments. She liked the harmony of a band dedicated to each other, working toward pleasant sounds. There was always something just right about the smooth Texas blues that was coming from the stage, as well.

Juneau slid a beer to her. "Ever tried the Blue Moon? It's pretty fantastic."

Caro looked around, on edge. "Are you kidding me? I'm not 21. There's no way you're 21, either!"

Juneau shrugged. "It's a college town. Half of the paying customers aren't 21, but the bar's gotta stay open." Caro sat up nervously, looking around. "Relax. Just don't go crazy, and you'll fit right in."

It was not that she'd never tried beer before. She occasionally sneaked light beer from her dad's refrigerator. It was always nasty. She assumed at some age that she would grow to love the taste. How else could people spend so much money drinking them all night?

The waitress came around to take orders and asked her if she wanted one. Caro froze, shaking her head slightly. The waitress brushed her red hair behind her, "Let me guess: water all night long?" Juneau pointed to her beer, held out two fingers and swept them on the table asking for another round. The waitress shrugged and walked away, returning with two more frosted goblets garnished with orange.

Caro's first sip was heavenly. "Are you sure this is beer?"

Juneau laughed. "Stick with me," she said as she took another long pull. "You've got a lot to learn about this town."

Caro sipped slowly on her beer until it warmed to just below room temperature. By that time, she didn't want anything else to do with it, and the heavy flavors filled her up to the point that she wasn't drunk, but she was full. She sat staring at the beer mug as she made casual conversation with JuJu until she was pulled out of her thoughts.

"What's going on? Got something on your mind?" Truth be told, she had plenty on her mind, but the one thing that kept her from relaxing and enjoying herself had been Chad bearing his feelings to her. She kept telling herself that it was fine, and as long as it was out there, they were better off, but she still couldn't get over the uncomfortable silence that hung in the air when he was around.

"Well, there's this guy…"

"Damn, girl. You don't waste time, do you?"

Caro put on a face like she had just tasted bitter cheese. "God, no. Far from it. This guy that's in engineering… he's professing his feelings for me."

"Didn't you just get here?"

"I KNOW." Caro wished there was a way she could explain this incredulity to Chad, or Evie even, but both of them seemed to think it was all perfectly natural.

"It's not like I can even pretend to be surprised. Do you know how many boys I've got begging me for phone numbers? Between classes, during class, hell, one boy asked to borrow a calculator and when he handed it back to me, there was a slip of paper in the back of it saying 'Will you go out with me? Check yes or no.'"

They laughed at the absurdity of it. "I just don't know what to tell him. I mean, I'm not into him, and even if I was, I don't speak Third Grade."

"I know, I just feel like I don't want to be too blunt, too vague, or too mean to this guy. I mean, he seems like a good kid. It was easier back home. Chris was always good for scaring away the competition." Juneau flinched, but Caro quickly corrected herself. "I mean, he would get jealous, sure, but never in any creepy way. It was just always the two of us, everywhere we went." She felt a guilty pang as the word 'us' rolled off her tongue. She had left him, and moved on to bigger and better things. He wouldn't have fit in here, she reminded herself. "I figure I was so eager to get out here and be on my own, I should learn to fight my own battles."

"Alright," Juneau ordered another beer. "You say this guy's a good kid, right?" Nods. "You say you don't want to be mean to him." Nods. "So, are you still hanging out with him?"

"Well, that's where it gets complicated. He's in my gaming group. We're meeting once a week."

"Oh, hold up. You mean to tell me that this guy sees you every week and you still can't find a way to tell him how you feel?"

Caro played with her napkin nervously. "Well, how am I supposed to know how I feel?"

"I can tell you right now. If you don't tell him you are not into him, you can count on getting asked out once a week until he finds a new infatuation. These engineering boys, especially the ones who haven't had much experience with girls, let me tell you that might be a while."

Caro couldn't argue the point. She also couldn't find a way to say what she was feeling, except that she didn't know him very well, and she wasn't sure if things would be better or worse if they tried going on a date. He certainly hadn't made the date any more tempting.

"So what are you telling him when he asks you out?"

"Not much, honestly. I don't know what I want, so I try not to lie, but I can't exactly say yes either, right?"

"Okay. So tell me why you don't want to date him."

"Because he's weird, and I feel like things will only get weirder if we go on a date."

Juneau smiled and took another sip of beer. "Good. Straight to the point, but he probably doesn't think he's weird, so what do you think you should tell him?"

"I don't know. I'd rather just leave things where they are. Maybe if he stops being so weird, I'll go on a date with him. How do I put that into words he'll understand?"

Juneau chuckled, "If I could tell you that, I'd be a rich woman." The sounds of the band were drowned out by a passing train, and they sat in silence while Caro contemplated her next move. It all seemed so obvious here, explaining everything to Juneau, but getting through to Chad seemed like a much bigger dragon to slay.

Caro shrugged it off. Chad would grow out of the crush, and things would settle down. Maybe after Christmas a new round of freshmen would come and he would soon forget why he tried so hard to impress her. She just needed to make sure she spent more nights like this, away from the confining crowd and around someone she could just be a girl around.

Juneau became the perfect outlet to get her out of the other crowd. Caro spent the entire first half of the semester within the confines of the dorms and classrooms. Off campus, Juneau introduced her into a world that thrived with music, food and drinks that she never discovered before. It felt freeing to be able to just be a girl with her, free of the confining conversations about dragons and special rules and which Doctor was the best, Tennant or Smith. The more time she spent shopping, dining and drinking, the more she drifted away from her dearest friends that at first made her feel so welcome.

One day before classes, Evie caught her on the way out the door. "What's up with you lately? It's like you've forgotten about us."

Caro felt the guilt that always nagged at her when she found peace and quiet out with Juneau. It was always fleeting, but it would invariably come back with the thought, 'Man, the guys would hate this.'

"I don't know. I've been venturing out into the real world, off campus on my own." Evie shot her a quizzical look. "I just wanted to try to do new things without the guys, you know?"

"You went to Taco Bell without us?"

"No! That's just it. There's more to do than just… fast food. Don't laugh, but, I've been shopping and…" she tried to find another way to put it, "doing girl stuff."

Evie was exasperated. "I can totally do girl stuff with you," she shot back. "I've got girl parts. I shop."

"Really?" Caro's voice was flat and cynical. "Okay, *girlfriend.*" She added heavy inflection to make sure her playful doubt came across clearly. "Why don't you come with us to Monroe this weekend? We're going to Sephora. I'll give you a clue: it's not a Final Fantasy character."

Evie rolled her eyes. "Believe it or not, roomie, I'm a girl just like you." She picked up her satchel and started toward the door. "Just because I game with you doesn't mean I don't like being included in girl stuff, too." She held one hand on the door, then turned to look at Caro again. "It doesn't have to be black and white, and besides, what if I needed to get away and be a girl for a night, too?" Evie shook her head and walked out, swinging the door closed behind her as she left.

The door slammed a little louder than she intended, but it echoed in Caro's head. Caro felt guilty for not even considering her roommate to be one of the girls. She'd introduced her to the guys, and had never put on makeup in all the time they shared a room. She never even talked about boys, or wine, or shoes, or anything like it. She sure hadn't helped to invite herself, and Caro tried to settle her conscience with that thought.

SEVEN

"I hope it's okay if I brought some friends." Caro had no idea that her trip to Monroe would turn into the caravan it became. She invited Evie over lunch in the cafeteria, but prying ears invited themselves along for the trip.

Juneau seemed happy to have Evie tag along. "Wow! Where'd you get those colors from?" She leaned in close to look at the funky blues and purples that the fair Norwegian used on her eyes. She touched the side of Evie's face to trace the jawline where, to Caro, Evie tried way too hard for an afternoon out on the town.

"Do you like it?" Evie batted her eyelashes. "I don't know. I guess I just never get to dress up. It's all charcoal and canvas in the art studio, and I heard there would be sushi." It felt a bit odd to Caro, seeing Evie this way. Suddenly, out from the dark dungeon, her roommate seemed to finally take an interest in dressing up like a girl the second Caro divulged her secret getaway from the guys. One guy, however, seemed hardest to get away from.

"I LOVE SUSHI," Aidan hung his arms over Caro and Evie's shoulders, eyes wide with excitement.

Juneau seemed unsure. "So… you're coming with us to town?" Aidan nodded. "…for clothes shopping, and makeup."

"I used to go shopping with my mom all the time," Aidan shrugged, "and I DO love sushi. Nothing in this town is served fresh. So," he arched his eyebrows, smiling wide, "are we in?"

Evie rolled her eyes. Caro felt a headache coming on. Juneau nodded in optimistic resignation. "Absolutely."

"I'm Aidan," he offered. Caro felt rude for not mentioning it earlier, but the hope lingered until a moment before that he still might not be coming.

"JuJu," she reached out and gave a firm handshake. When Caro eyed her curiously, she repeated, "My friends call me JuJu."

At the clothing store, Aidan was surprisingly helpful. "I have to admit," Caro said as they dug through clearance racks of fall colors on the cusp of winter, "when you told us that you shopped with your mom, I figured you'd recommend stuff for us that would make us look like an old woman."

"I may be… attached to my family—"

"Mama's boy," Evie called out from behind a dressing room door.

"—but I know what I like on a woman, and it has nothing to do with my MOTHER." He angled his voice toward Evie's changing room door, just for good measure. Shaking his head, he perused a nearby rack before finding an orange and brown blouse with a swooping neck, holding it up to Caro's shoulders. Her brown hair shined, hanging loosely over the cotton weave. He smiled in appreciation. "That one's yours. Go go go." He shooed, leading her into another dressing room.

JuJu stepped out from behind the far dressing room door in a black dress, with sequins dressing up a sheer fabric that extended from her low neckline to the nape of her neck. In her best Marilyn Monroe, she cooed, "What do ya think, stud?"

Aidan held his hand to his chin, thinking. Caro giggled at the thought that real people actual do that while thinking. Without a word, he strode to an accessory rack with hands out, like a composer before a symphony. He pulled a dark purple scarf from the rack, felt its soft texture and nodded. He almost skipped over to her, presenting it between two closed fists. "If you can pull the scarf from the stone, you will be its rightful heir." She giggled in the tug of war, coming out victorious.

"Anybody ever tell you you're pretty awesome?"

A hush fell behind the other two dressing room doors. The girls whispered to each other in giddy tones.

"I had an uncle like you, you know?"

Aidan looked down at his collection of clothes and accessories, and then blushed. "I'm not... you know... No... I mean–"

"Oh – I don't... I mean. No! I just mean my uncle was a, a... well." She realized it had started to sound really bad, and just shrugged. "A nerd."

"You're surrounded by engineering students. We're all nerds."

"Nah. Not like the good kinds." She grabbed a hat from the rack, putting it on her head and staring into the mirror. "Most of the guys here try so hard to be something different. They put on clothes that don't match their inside. They compete in these silly battles over who's got the biggest brain, or who's got the bigger muscles."

She looked at him dead on now. Steady eye contact made him nervous. "People like you are rare. You seem to genuinely love the skin you're in."

Aidan shook his head. "It's all I've got to work with."

"Me?" JuJu turned back to the mirror, "I'd change a dozen things about the skin I'm in before I really felt comfortable. I'd start with the hips." The other three laughed at that, and then Juneau got serious. "You know they tell me the same thing they told my uncle? When my white friends tried to bring up black people, I'd get really uncomfortable and they'd see it. They told me… They told me 'It's fine, JuJu. You're not really black.'"

Caro cringed. "Sounds like some pretty rotten friends, if you ask me."

"What can I do? It feels like I have to choose. I can go to college, build computers, or fit some stupid person's expectations."

"Looks like you're doing a great job just being you," Aidan said. "You're not just anything. Not just a nerd. Not just a black woman. You're all of it," he chucked her on her shoulder for good measure, "and small minds will never be able to make that fit into their worldview."

Juneau sighed. "Whatever. Let's get some sushi. I'm starving."

As they checked out, Caro thought back on fighting to be more than just a girl in a boy's major. She pitied the girl who fought two stereotypes, even though Juneau managed it pretty well. Despite how bright she was in Math classes, Caro dreaded how a day with her and the upperclassman might go. She realized she'd misjudged on too many levels, herself. She didn't have the girls' day all to herself. She brought Evie along out of guilt, and ended up having lots of fun with her three new shopping buddies.

It was barely 4:30 when they arrived at the sushi restaurant. The best restaurant in Monroe had amazing reviews, but Caro expected very little when she recalled living near the coast just a few months previously, in a much bigger city. Dark wood booths lined the sides of the restaurant, and Japanese wall scrolls stretched out periodically along the back and front walls. A long blue aquarium greeted them as they walked up to the front podium, and they were greeted by an old Asian lady.

They opted for a spot at the bar, even though no other tables were being used. Caro loved the sight of fresh fish in the glass in front of her, and no one else seemed to mind. Aidan sat at the corner of the sushi bar, with Juneau next to him so she could sit next to Caro as well. Caro made sure to get a seat next to Evie. She tried to make sure that Evie understood that she was welcome, and she figured Aidan could handle himself as far as dinner conversation with his new friend.

Aidan sat in front of the menu cascading fingers together in a maniacal fit of glee. JuJu looked over his shoulder and recommended some of her favorites.

"Oh, I've got this." When the sushi chef asked for drinks, Aidan rambled off an order in Japanese. The chef rolled his eyes, moving on to Juneau. By the time everyone's order was placed, a small crowd began to trickle in.

From behind the bar, a tall blond guy with short curly hair stepped out in a white shirt and a tie. Caro hunched her shoulders when recognition sunk in. How could he be here?

Chris was almost past her before he shuffled his feet to a halt. "Babe, what are you doing here?"

Evie jumped to her rescue while Caro sat dumbstruck. "We just had to try this spot. I hear it's the best sushi spot around."

Without taking his eyes off of Caro, Chris nodded. "I hear they're looking for a new manager. I actually just finished interviewing." Chris crossed his fingers. "It looks like I might have a new job to help make ends meet now that I'm up here, too."

"You're… in Monroe?" Caro's eyes narrowed while she tried to process the new information.

"No. When you started this new life, I figured if I wanted to be a part of it I'd enroll here, too. Monroe isn't too far, so I'll be able to work weekends, and maybe pick up a few shifts during the week as well. I'm in a general studies program now." Chris smiled big, "I'm in college." He pulled a chair up to join them, but hesitated when she didn't respond. "That's what you wanted, wasn't it?"

Caro wanted a fresh start most of all as she started to plan for the future. Seeing a familiar face was nice, even if the last time she had seen him was on such rough terms. "I figured you'd hate me. Why follow me?"

"Because it mattered to you."

Evie was the first to break the silence among the rest of the group. "So Caro, aren't you going to introduce us to your boyfriend?"

"He's not my boyfriend." Ouch. That came out harsher than she wanted. She felt the acidity hang in the air. Her eyes turned soft, and she bit her lip as she took in the awkwardness of the whole situation. She wanted to thank him. Having a piece of home follow her felt like too much of a godsend to discount, so she tried to at least make him feel as welcome as she could. "If you're all done, why don't you join us? Everybody, this is Chris."

Caro tapped Evie on the leg and the two exchanged hushed words. With a quick shove, Caro nudged Evie by the hip off of the sushi barstool, and waved Chris over. "Why don't you sit here," she turned to face Evie as she finished her idea, "between us."

Ding. Evie followed suit. "Yeah, totally. Plenty of room on this side. How come I never see you on campus?"

"Oh, I'm just getting settled. I still haven't moved all my furniture from my parents' place down in LaPlace." His Cajun accent thickened the more he talked about the small South Louisiana town. "We just finished the first run this weekend. We're headed back next Friday."

"My God, just keep talking." Evie laid a menu between her and Caro.

"I'm sorry?" Chris was clueless, and Caro tried to hide her surprise at Evie's enthusiasm.

"Uh… IT'S – Yeah, IT'S a crazy accent you've got there. Where did you say it was from?"

"LaPlace. Well, that's where my family's from anyway."

Caro's eyes went wide as she looked at Evie and mouthed slowly, "What are you doing?" Chris made his way over between the two girls. "Yeah, that's great. So how's Mama and them doing?"

JuJu suppressed a giggle and flicked her straw paper at the two girls, "Calm down. You two are going full retard over this boy."

Caro blushed as he sat down, and did her best to regain her composure. She struggled to change the subject. "We were just talking about our new engineering project," she said.

"We were?" Aidan was confused.

"Yeah. Well, I'm in engineering now, and JuJu and I've been talking to Aidan and these boys about their projects, because I've got to come up with something for a freshman project.

"That's wonderful," he said. He hung on her every word. Caro had never remembered him being such an intense listener. "What is the project?"

Caro fell flat. "I have no idea. Every suggestion is just so boring."

JuJu chimed in, "I'd give anything to make something Professor Dietrich's never seen. Everything's been done, though."

Aidan giggled from his end of the bar, "How many doggy door projects this year?"

"None!" Caro's frustration spilled out on the sushi bar. "It was on the list – this list of all these projects that everyone's done before. We've got nothing but a list of things we can't do, and it just feels like there's nothing new that can be done."

"Do not despair," Aidan offered with a flourish. "You've got the king of the ring on your side."

"This man," Evie pointed to the end of the sushi bar, "this man took your little robots and made a boxing game out of it." JuJu shook her head. The 'robots' could barely be called that. With limited inputs and a miniscule programming memory, nothing they programmed worked on more than two or three tasks in a single uploaded code. The programs themselves were so limited, it would take such a dense code.

"99% of the programmable memory and 97% of the storage memory." Aidan nodded his head. "I barely got away with it."

"What do you mean?" It didn't sound to Caro as if he broke any rules.

"The hard part for most people is making a sensor interact with the robot," Aidan admitted. "For me, the hard part was selling my professors on the idea that a game solved a world problem."

Caro tried to stand. A thought exploded in her mind, opening pathways and suggesting futures and washing away doubts about the next step. As soon as she slid off the stool, though, her ankle twisted and she felt a sickening crack. She dropped like a sack of potatoes, her plate of sushi untouched and her crowd of friends trying to catch her before she hit the ground.

When she came to, she was on the back seat of JuJu's Explorer and Chris managed a small splint from white napkins and chopsticks. "Calm down," he soothed her. "We're almost to the hospital."

"I just had this idea," she felt like she was shouting, but no one heard her. "I know what I want to design." The car jolted to a stop, and Juneau honked her horn, swearing at a reckless driver. The sudden stop pushed her ankle into Chris, seated on the floorboard in front of her. Needles shot up her leg, back, and down her arms. She screamed. Just like that, the thought disappeared.

Coming out of the hospital, she struggled to make the crutches work with her. Juneau and Chris coaxed her toward the maroon Explorer, and Aidan was holding a Styrofoam plate out to her. "It seemed a shame to waste. Another hour and I would have had to finish it."

Caro sighed and smiled gratefully. She opened up her special roll with avocado and ate it gingerly the whole way home. Chris eyed her fish suspiciously. "This looks terrible."

She passed him a bite and he nodded in agreement. "Yes. Terrible fish. I'm sorry you had to wait so long for it. You deserve a do-over when you're ready. Sushi, Part 2, same time next week?"

She had her reservations about what Chris thought it might mean. After everything had calmed down, though, she was impressed with this new Chris, and having someone here who knew her, like really knew her, was nice. "A do over sounds nice."

EIGHT

"Are you just going to sit there in your bed all week?"

"NOT HAPPENING."

It had been four days since the sushi incident. Caro had no intention of being out of bed more than she needed. She managed around campus, hobbling from class to class, bringing enough food back at the end of the school day to sustain her until the next morning. She had done little outside the confines of her small dorm room that was beyond what was required of her. She preferred it that way. She didn't see much reason to work for it. She had her weekends, and her gaming group would survive just fine without her for a few weeks until she healed up. The bed was confining, and the room was stuffy, but the more she could heal over the week, the better she might be prepared for next week's date.

A date. She knew that Chris might see it as starting over their relationship, or as starting over a friendship. She had no idea which she wanted more. On top of that was the odd way that Evie had started to react when she found out that Chris and Caro were exes. She thought of little else since she broke her foot. He checked in on her through text daily. Evie constantly asked what would become of it, saying that if Caro wasn't going to take him up on his offer, that Evie would do something about it. Evie only pushed harder when Caro insisted that Chris was only ever going to be a friend. Caro pushed the idea one night, and Evie just shrugged and told her that she just wanted her roomie to be happy.

Now Evie came to her with an ultimatum: to get out of bed and attend a social event with her or wallow in misery alone. Evie brought up the possibility of moving out until Caro healed up rather than watch her sulk around the dorm. Caro didn't think she would do it, but took her brusque attempts at socializing her as a loving concern for her well-being. It hardly counted as a social event, anyway. The university's anime club met every week to ignore each other in public as weird, incomprehensible cartoons flashed across the screen. She had seen a few when she was younger. It was twice as random as Family Guy, and half as entertaining.

"At least show up for the first part of the meeting. They're ordering pizza. That means lots of new people to meet!"

It didn't sound like a bad idea, but Caro wondered how meeting someone over a type of entertainment that didn't interest her would go.

"PLEEEEAAASSSE."

It didn't seem that waiting Evie out was going to work, and this was probably as persuasive as it was going to get. Everything after Evie resorted to begging would likely be annoying, and getting in the way of a good nap.

"Mediocre pepperoni pizza and scatterplot cartoons? Where do I sign up?"

"We pass a sign-in sheet every week. I'll make sure it gets to you."

Sarcasm was beyond the faithfully initiated. She learned about scatterplots in her engineering classes. The idea that you could take several points of interest and graph them to determine a pattern was hardly the reason why she gave the anime genre its nickname. No, what bothered her the most about the cartoons was its inability to keep one cohesive storyline for long, at least from what she had seen. The 'scatterplot' she saw when she looked at the randomness much more resembled the scattershot of a shotgun, which favored quantity over quality in the hopes of hitting the widest fan base possible. She disliked many things that sacrificed story for aesthetics.

When she had properly been escorted to the anime night, she saw Aidan giving a brief overview of five shows that they previously agreed that the club wanted to watch. There were lots of comparisons and inside jokes meant to sway people to one show or another, but none of them made any sense to her. When they finally settled on some kind of zombie, ninja, pirate cheerleader cartoon, she was grateful that the inside jokes were over, and she didn't have to pretend to be listening. As the lights went out, she felt a rocking in the row of stadium chairs where she sat. "Look who's back from the dead."

She rolled her eyes at the sudden appearance of Chad. He had backed off considerably after the misunderstanding at the game, but she didn't know what to think of him anymore. She wondered if he was able to be just friends with girls, but decided to save her judgment for another day. Familiar voices weren't so bad to hear after all.

"Careful, I might be a zombie cheerleader ninja hungry for braaiins." She let the words creep out softly trying to make the joke without disturbing the serious fans. "Oh, is that you, Chad? Never mind. You're safe."

He chuckled under his breath. "Yep. I deserve that."

"No, I didn't mean–"

"Nah, forget it. I'm clueless about girls. No surprise there." He propped his feet up and relaxed. Caro tried to remember the last time she had seen him relaxed. "I'm good now. I've spent some time thinking, and I've come to a conclusion." Oh? "There will be a girl to come along who has as much experience dating as I have, and then maybe, MAYBE she'll be willing to make the same mistakes with me that the rest of you have been making for a decade. I can handle that. I can wait. I get it."

He was certainly taking it well. "Did Evie talk to you?"

"Nah, Aidan had a few words to say, though."

"Aidan?" Caro had a hard time imagining Aidan giving good advice. They must have been closer than she realized. "Well," she breathed a little sigh of relief, and gratitude, "good. I'm sure she'll be a lucky girl."

Chad talked to her for a little while longer in hushed tones, asking about her pain medicines and coping with class schedules. The genuine interest and steady conversation was a pleasant blessing. Less than thirty minutes flew by and the episode was over, and the debate began anew for which story would be next. Chad excused himself to join in the discussion, and the lights went out again.

Alone… -ish in the dark, she felt her pain medicine kicking in as the random images flashed across the screen. Evie sat beside her, making side comments with each new revelation in the story as she tried to help Caro catch up. Caro thought she saw a demon, and maybe there was a girl in a short skirt. It seemed like there was always a schoolgirl in a short skirt. Her eyes got heavy.

She was on the edge of a great red cliff, sitting with her feet hanging over the ledge. The cliff overlooked a great blue and white castle in the distance with a dozen high towers and a great wall surrounded another city safely nestled within. The wind blew through her hair, and she saw Chris in the corner of her eye. Standing a few feet away, one foot brushing dangerously close to the edge, Chris was dressed in royal robes and held a sheathed rapier at his side. He looked out over the edge of the cliff without acknowledging her presence, at first unwilling to break the palpable silence.

The wind howled, pushing them closer to the edge as he pulled a brass key from a leather string around his neck. Chris tossed the key casually to her. Without saying a word, he held an open hand palm up toward the horizon. She played with the teeth of the key, trying to imagine if it opened a door to the castle, the gate to the great wall, or some mysterious treasure hidden somewhere within. He offered no clue. He stepped closer and ran a hand through her hair. It was warm, and it tickled her ear. That was weird. She was used to seeing the winds, foods and scenery of her dreams. Feeling was new.

She opened her eyes and realized that someone's hands were running through her hair. She let out a short, sharp scream as she jumped back. Everyone stopped and turned to look at her. Everyone was looking except for Evie, who still sat beside her and looked down at the ground. A giggle passed through the crowd as they returned to their show and Evie relaxed.

Caro talked out of the side of her mouth, trying to avoid eye contact and unsure of where the conversation might go. "Touching my hair? Um… is there something I should know?"

"I dunno." Evie's shrugging apology was visible even in the dimly lit room. "Maybe. Sorry. I was just… you know… just enjoying the show, uh, anime."

"Maybe you're sorry or maybe I should know something?" Caro didn't want to know the answer. She got up and hobbled out of the room. Evie followed close behind.

"You looked like you were enjoying it. Were you?" She played with her hands, looking up only occasionally to gauge Caro's reaction.

Caro remembered the feeling, but also remembered the source in her dreams. "That doesn't matter. You can't DO that to somebody. You can't just help yourself to someone when they're sleeping." Her mixed feelings bubbled over from confusion to anger. "You can't… God. You're worse than Chad."

"I just didn't know how to tell you, and you looked so peaceful."

"At least Chad didn't know any better."

"Yeah, and I'm a chicken." Evie's voice carried through the empty hallways. The late night showing of the anime club meant the entire building of classrooms was abandoned, save the auditorium where they were given access to the sound and video equipment. The good news was that there would be no one to hear them, except for a group of people engrossed in loud, random and attention-grabbing shows.

Evie let her emotions settle while Caro waited for an apology. None was forthcoming. "You know what happens when Chad tells a girl he likes them? She laughs it off, and we laugh it off. You know what happens when I tell someone I like them?"

Caro shook her head in frustration, throwing her hands out in protest and waiting for more.

"Seriously, do you have any idea what happens when I tell someone I like them? Because it hasn't happened. I'm out on a limb, dealing with something I've never put out there. It just feels like I'm running out of time. You've got this big date coming up with your old flame, and I just… I feel like I've only got one shot to explain how I feel before you go running back to him." She took another step closer for consolation, "And I'm scared as hell."

Caro knew the feeling, but the smell of betrayal was fresh on her hair, her ears.

"I wasn't trying to hurt you," Evie confessed. "I admit I was trying to surprise you. I figured you might laugh it off, or you might just have a moment of honesty where I could tell what you really thought about me." Evie took another step until she was arm's length away from Caro. Her arms fidgeted looking for embrace, for a consoling hug or something, any kind of sign of acceptance. Caro didn't want to be accepting. She didn't like surprises.

"What do you want from me, Evie?" Caro grasped for a reasoning behind tonight's invasion. "There's nothing here between us to tell you I want anything more than a roommate."

"Are you sure?"

This girl was dense. "Yup. I'm pretty damn sure." Evie took another step closer, until they were nearly nose to nose. In all her anger and confusion, Caro could still feel the hand that ran through her hair. It didn't feel so bad that it had been the one person that helped her feel welcome at this new, big, and strange school. Evie's lips touched Caro's. It was electric, comforting, loving and sincere.

"Didn't see that coming," Aidan's voice called from the open doorway. At the door leading to the anime room, Aidan and Chad looked on at the scene unfolding. Evie backed away, blushing and exposed, and nothing greater than shock managed to show on Caro's face. "How do you like that, Chad? We get two girls in the gaming group, they go for each other."

"THIS IS BULLSHIT." Chad stormed out of the building. He kicked the door open out of some need for more emphasis on the unfairness of it all, punctuating the slamming of the door into the outside wall with another expletive for good measure, "BULLSHIT."

NINE

Caro had never seen Lars so alert. He circled around the table, working through the problems the rest of the group worked through a half an hour before. Tomorrow was the midterm, and Lars had a long way to go to catch up with the rest of the class. The rest of the class, Caro included, were already skating on thin ice. She couldn't imagine the kind of miracle that he would need to pull off to make it out of the class and on to the next semester.

"Okay, for the salt dilution problem," Patrick sketched rough figures and worked through the first set of equations. "This is how we did it in class. What if he makes the size of the water jug the variable? How would we work through that?" Patrick had been relentless, pushing every boundary, switching every problem up, and throwing curveballs like a major league pitcher.

"No way. He wouldn't do that, would he?" Lars paced nervously. "How did you get this answer in homework three?" He held out the original page from the notebook of assignments, in pristine condition. Patrick was patient as ever, even though Caro couldn't understand why. As Patrick started working through the problem from his neatly assembled binder, Lars copied the steps and stood back, satisfied.

"You're going to have to try a lot harder than that," Juneau worked through some formulas on the side as she kept one ear bud in. The rest of the table heard the faint echoes of white noise coming from her headset. Caro strained to differentiate between waves, rain, or both. It was already well past dinner, and the engineering college was full of students getting settled in. Aidan and Wil were down the hall in one of the regular classrooms, working at the desks that had the table and chair all-in-one. Aidan told Caro to be prepared, because there would be dozens of people huddled up in the building through dawn. She believed him, because the way that bunch never took chances worked for them so far.

What surprised her most, though, was the people who weren't there. The people who always turned in their work on time. The people who never struggled through homework problems and solicited help or inspiration from the rest of the class. The people who seemed to have everything all worked out were strangely not present. The majority of the freshmen and older students were all there, though. Many had laptops running with music, games or videos going. The international students set up their own corner near the door where they talked amongst themselves. The more she looked at the study materials, the more she wanted to switch her major. She wondered how many of the English majors were up all night preparing for an exam. Evie was in the dorm room, playing video games and playing catchup with her family. From what she gathered, all of the art students' deadlines came at the end of the semester. She wasn't sure if she'd want it that way, but right now the option to get some sleep sounded awfully nice.

By midnight, most of the crowds had cleared out. Lars said that he didn't perform well on no sleep, so he went to bed. Patrick had kids to take care of, so he left around ten to make sure they were asleep. "I don't have it," Caro whimpered. "I'm going to fail, go home, and just be homeless. Is that okay?"

Juneau smirked from under a pile of papers. "Homelessness doesn't sound so bad…" she mouthed the word again, "homelessness… is that even a word?"

"I don't know. Ask an English major. My brain is mush." Caro scribbled more notes onto the printouts of the past six weeks. Greek letters started to blend together. Numbers mushed into one another. She picked up her phone and texted Wil an SOS, and everything went dark.

Caro woke to the pounding of a basketball. It felt like it was bouncing against her head. Somewhere between the coffee, sugar and energy drinks, she figured she'd gone too far. She squinted to the table that used to have the loudest group, but they had all gone home. Aidan and Wil stood in the doorway, dribbling. "I must be dreaming."

"Why else would I be here?" Aidan gave the best double-shooter hand gesture he could muster toward her. "Your hero has arrived."

"Oh, God, it's a nightmare."

"No, come on." Wil dribbled into the study room. The carpet muffled the sound slightly, but still not enough to keep away the pounding in her head.

"Do you really have to?"

"Physical activity reminds the body that I'm awake. Everybody's got a trick." Wil rolled a chair up to her table and started looking at the problems. "Ew. No fun, but not impossible. Where do you think you stand on all of this?"

"Somewhere between failing and failing miserably." Caro banged her head on the table. Some of the throbbing of her temples faded, so she did it again for good measure.

Juneau got up and brought her binder to a huge dry erase board. Other than four people at a table on the other side, they were the only ones left in the biggest of the engineering classrooms. She started on one end, writing down all the equations they went through, and then worked her way to the other end where she started writing down the questions from the homework sheets. While Wil walked Caro through one of the later problems, they looked up to see Juneau connecting dots on the board.

"What are you doing?"

"Just trying to work it out. Could he make us use the equations here," she reaches up and starts a big blue dry erase line at the top of the board, "to solve for something we don't know here." She finished her big blue line somewhere near the bottom. The clock ticked loudly as the dread set in Caro's stomach.

"I sure as hell hope not." Caro really didn't want to think about it. "I just want to be able to answer these questions by memory. If we start connecting dots, we'll never–"

"No, she's onto something." Wil came up to the board and grabbed a red marker. He lined from the third problem down to somewhere around the fifteenth. "This one looks familiar."

"We don't have time to go through every possible scenario." She looked out the window to see the first sliver of light on the horizon. We've got two hours, and I'm running on empty."

The doors burst open with the smell of donuts. Lars walked in, hair unbrushed and eyes half open, "Crunch time, kids. I think I can help."

Caro couldn't see how he could hurt. They gave him three to work through on his side of the board while Caro and Juneau worked through four each. Wil and Aidan bounced their basketball down the hallways as they left for their last push before their midterms began, confident they could make more headway.

The best blessing that they could have asked for was that they didn't have to move when it was finally time to take the midterm. They placed themselves intentionally in the class they would be taking their exam. When the morning class started to wander in, they were grateful for their decision. Caro doubted she could have gone far, and she definitely couldn't have driven to class had she stayed too far away from campus the night before.

Professor Dietrich walked in, bringing a wave of sickly sweet aftershave with him. He took special notice of the table of donuts and misfits hard at work. "Mr. Lars. I see you making an effort today. Glad to have you."

Juneau and Caro looked up from their paperwork and smiled weakly. Every move was molasses. Every thought was lead. Caro managed a pitiful, "Morning, professor."

"Still think you've got what it takes?"

"I'm... sorry?"

"Get over it, Caro. You'll never pass this class. You might as well go home. Your grades stink as bad as your project–"

Caro shook herself awake to a full classroom and Professor Dietrich handing out the exams. "Put your notes away, everyone." Somewhere between alertness and exhaustion, she struggled to sift through what she must have dreamed.

She looked down to a chaotic mess of papers and pencils and a dry erase marker that she had miraculously opened and marked across her forearms. She was pretty sure there was marker on her face, too, but she would have to wait to find out.

Her cold sweats eased a little as she started to look at the test. She expected the midterm to be a nightmarish cryptic Rosetta stone filled with messages that made no sense. Instead, she recognized many of the problems that they worked through after dawn. She took a quick peek at Lars next to her, who worked solidly through the problem set. Other than the small tapping of his foot, he seemed in good spirits. Juneau was doing well, too. Patrick was on the other side of her, and a cardboard barrier stood between them in a big x around the table. The two hour test was finished in just under an hour and a half, and Caro felt much of the anxiety melt away. It was quickly replaced with the exhaustion of a draining exam and the all-nighter that she had yet to pay for. She hobbled back to her dorm on her crutches and slept the rest of the day away. Regular classes could wait. For now, sleeping through them felt like her little victory dance. When she woke up at suppertime, she found an email waiting for her from Professor Dietrich. She knew that she hadn't been doing well lately, but she figured she blew him away with her last test results until she found out why he wanted to talk to her. She spent that night barely eating, barely sleeping. She didn't feel like she wanted either. She didn't want to "discuss her grade," either, as he suggested. She laid in her bed and waited until his office opened the next morning.

When she arrived the next day, she was grateful to have escaped the stress headache, but would have done anything to avoid smelling that aftershave that just reminded her of his condescending tone and that he expected a significant portion of his class to fail. She hardly felt like a contributing member of the deserving, passing portion. She stepped into the crowded office and tried to appear at ease. A sinking feeling set in when he turned to greet her.

"Well, Miss Caro, have you thought about what you're going to turn in for your final project?" Professor Dietrich looked at her from over the top of his glasses. Her heart beat faster, and she tried not to think about the slew of unanswered question from the previous day's exam. She didn't like being in faculty offices. It felt too disciplinary, like a bad meeting with a high school principal. It helped a little that she spent so much time in Dr. Hu's office, but only a little. Professor Dietrich's workspace was much less inviting. Professional journals and manila folders stacked high on each side, looming over the two of them like a dizzying mountain. The top of his desk was barely visible under the stacks of papers, and on the top of the stack was her midterm.

Professor Dietrich reached for it and held it in his hand. "Good work, young lady. You're improving, but–"

The word caught in her brain. She braced herself for the worst.

She couldn't imagine trying harder. If she tried any harder, she'd... she'd...

She started crying, and he set her paper down where the glaring red D hung between them. "You can do it. I know you can. This engineering thing, it's not for everyone. Hey. If it doesn't work out this quarter, there's always next." It didn't feel like compassion. It didn't feel like encouragement. It felt like a plea to give up, pack her bags and get out.

She walked out the door and headed down the hallway. He called out to her as she got halfway to the exit. "You can still knock the project out of the park."

TEN

The days got awkward in the dorm. Evie only slept in the room now and waited as late as possible before finally showing up. Most of those nights, Caro had already been asleep, or faked sleep to avoid talking about it. Chad wasn't handling it very well, but neither was Caro. She was sure she hadn't done anything to give Evie an indication that she was interested. The kiss was nice, but not in any kind of an earth-shattering way that made her rethink things between them, or rethink the upcoming sushi date with Chris when Saturday rolled around. Caro managed that Saturday morning as best as she could, working around her cast to go shopping for a new dress. Trying on clothes was difficult enough, but she didn't like the way anything looked on her. Nothing fit quite right, or sent the right message. She didn't even know what she wanted the message to say. In the end, she picked out a black and white dress she always loved, and hadn't worn in far too long. Dresses were just easier while she still wore the cast, and she was grateful for that.

She met him a little after six at the local Japanese restaurant. He walked in wearing a button-down silk shirt and a black sports coat, walking briskly and smiling warmly. "Sorry I'm late," he said as he started to slide into the bench across from her in the black and green booth. He saw that her foot was propped up and instead scooted onto the same bench that she sat on. She hadn't realized her foot might be in the way. She started to apologize, but his familiar sandalwood cologne wafted over to her from where he was sitting, and she decided she liked the proximity.

"I have so much that I want to talk to you about," he offered as the waitress brought them their drinks. "I am still learning about all this dragon stuff. It's fascinating."

"Dragon stuff?"

"Yeah, I hear that's all you talk about these days. It's fine, really. I never paid enough attention before, but I'm here now." He pulled a yellow daisy from an inner coat pocket, putting it in his water and sliding the glass toward her. She blushed, realizing that he must have called her mother, because he had never remembered before. She filed that conversation with her mom away for a later time.

It sounded like something Aidan would say, and she could only guess at what else he had been told. "No. I don't talk about just dragons. There's lots more, even though I like the game."

"Dungeons and Dragons, right? You make them call you master?"

"What? Who told you that? Aidan?"

"Aidan? Nah. That other guy told me that I would have to dress up as well, that I'd have to suit up and fight dragons in the woods with you if I was serious."

She seethed somewhere between rage and contempt. "Let me guess." She took a deep breath, holding her head in her hands, "Chad?"

As if he pulled a rabbit out of his hat, his agreement came quickly. "That's the one. Great guy. He told me all kinds of other things about you. I admit, I'm no good at casting magic spells. I'll try, though, for you."

He was trying, she had to admit. His gullible streak would need some improvement. She would have to speak to Chad soon, as well. "No, you don't have to. Really. That's not how it–"

Chris' eyes pouted. He came into the conversation so prepared, but he felt his control of the situation slipping. "How does this world of yours work? I'm so sorry. I've never asked."

She breathed deeply, starting over. "Where do you go when you read a book? Not, like, your room. Where does your mind go?"

"I go to the Andes," he explained. Low lights and paper lanterns gave way to stone floors and a rocky path. A small house on the side of a mountain sprouted in the distance. "I found these pictures once in a National Geographic," he began. Tall, skinny trees shot up into the air, extending rapidly one after another up the mountainous slopes of Argentina. Small wooden posts marked the way as travelers passed by bus and car where once they had only walked up the narrow paths barefoot. "It was the most beautiful thing I'd ever seen. I told myself I'd see them in person one day."

Caro leaned back to take in the greens and browns of the mountains. "Do you think you'll ever get there?"

"Yes." He was giddy with excitement now. He grabbed her hand and looked directly into her eyes. "I'll make it there. You'll see. I want to take you with me."

"You've got a long way to go."

"I'll make it. You'll see." Chris looked up to the peaks high above. "Nothing comes cheaply here. I have to admit, I don't think I could have done any of this without you. You've really inspired me to do more." She had to admit that nothing came cheaply here. She was lucky to have the inheritance that her father left her. She knew that his family hadn't saved for him to go back to college, so she could only imagine what kind of loans he might be taking to come all this way to join her.

The sushi arrived to the table, bringing them out of the woody smells of the mountains. A wafting smell of miso soup hit her nose as the path returned to the dark wood benches where they sat, "But make no mistake, Caro: everything that I left behind? It's all been worth it."

She blushed, sure that in spite of the great leaps he had taken to get out of his old rut and transition into college mode, this was about her. No one their age had ever done so much just for her. Sure, her dad had moved heaven and earth to make sure she was taken care of, but how far would this boy... this man go to be there for her after he had picked up and moved like this? "I don't know, Chris. I half expected that when I left, you'd settle down with a local girl, just live on in the real world while I go and chase my imaginary one."

"Tell me about your world," he offered. "Tell me what's so great about it, then. Tell me where you run off to when you're not running off to classes."

Unwilling to go anywhere without her sushi, she carried the fancy plate of tuna and sticky rice with her into the royal castle around which everything in Rillis revolved. Her escapism was good for getting away from stresses in her schoolwork, anxiety about new crowds, but in small town sushi, she found something beautiful worth bringing into her sanctuary. Sushi plate in hands, she wandered the great alabaster halls of the great castle, laying out epic artwork of heroic deeds and running her hands along the reds and yellows in the stained glass.

Chris followed closely behind, hands in pockets. "This is amazing. Did you make all of this?"

"Most of it. I spent the last few months of my senior year putting together maps and histories." They walked into a grand dining hall where a feast was being held. "Most of the people in here are from my life back home. Shadows of bad teachers, or all the best parts of the people that I love."

They walked up to the end of the table, where a red-headed wise man sat in contemplative silence, his royal robes spilling over the sides of the gilded throne. A great feast spread before him, but he only drank deep from a silver goblet of red wine. Chris walked up to the table, popping a date in his mouth. "Wow. He looks as amazing as ever."

"Dad?" She cocked her head in surprise. "That's new. I mean, there was never a king here before. He must have snuck in when I moved away." She moved closer to get a good look. "When I was growing up, we always had our fantasy games to bring us closer together. Even when times were tough in high school," she crossed her arms and looked down, "when you weren't there or helpful, I would visit with him in my head sometimes. I admit I haven't visited him much since I moved here. I guess I just got too busy."

"Does he, will he talk to us?"

"Well, kind of. I mean, I could always see him in my head. Just... start a conversation. Deep inside, I always know what he's going to say about, well, pretty much anything." She fidgeted, absent-mindedly picking a few grapes from the table and dropping them to the floor. "I always had his graveside, so he was still there for me in a weird way, right?"

"And how long has it been since you visited him here?"

"This is new." It was more than the addition of her father, though. The whole inside of the castle was new. More doors appeared in the grand hall than she remembered from her sketchbook. New tapestries lined the walls, depicting epic deeds with her father, or her, or in some places someone vaguely resembling Chris. She thought about the dream, and the key that Chris held in it. "Why did you bring me here?"

"To eat?" Chris shrugged. "You looked like you were enjoying your meal until you fell. I figured you deserved a do-over. Besides, I get ten percent off here."

"Not the restaurant. Why did you bring me here, inside the castle?"

"Ah, now you might be stretching. I'm genuinely curious about you, and the worlds that you make. I just wanted to see the world for myself, but I didn't bring you here. You brought me."

Caro sighed as she looked at the gorgeous castle, the beautiful *landscape of her made up world. She considered what it might be like to go back to her dorm, back to her classes. "I don't want to go home."*

"What is waiting for you at home?"

She realized she referred to her dorm room for the first time ever as 'home', though it was far from that. "Stupid roommate. Stupid school. Stupid project." She dreaded the path that each took her on. Her classes progressed nicely enough, but very little headway had been made on her engineering project, which felt more like a glorified baking soda volcano than some inventive way to use a mass-produced, ubiquitous light sensor.

"I guess I just thought I'd be making great things when they told me we were designing something for engineering classes. I guess I thought I'd have the tools to make something beautiful, something more like this."

"Why not?"

"Why not make something like this?" She looked around at the hall. With her sushi done, and the banquet finished, everyone left but her king and father, and the remains of the meal lay strewn about the table and floor. Nothing looked particularly like chips and circuitry. Her robot barely controlled the servos that motored it around the mini mazes her professors designed for them. The four AA batteries that powered the unit seemed so small and insignificant. She struggled for the words, but nothing came out. No argument seemed to address anything. She just shook her head 'no' and shrugged the idea away. "Engineering doesn't work like that."

"What's the problem?"

"I miss him." Caro was standing in front of her father now,

passed out on the table from the feast. "We built the worlds that made high school bearable. I'm on my own, now. I make a world for four people, and one of them probably won't talk to me anymore. I'm losing one of the few friends I've made, and I don't know how to–" she tried again to push the thought of Evie out of her mind.

"It sounds to me like you've got a real problem." He picked up an apple from the table, throwing it into a corner. A pair of bull mastiffs chased after it, fighting with bear-like growls and playful head butts.

"How did you–"

"You're not alone. The boys, they help you build your world just by being there. They can create just as well as you."

"I still don't see how this fixes my problem."

Chris grabbed her by her shoulders, gripping her firmly. "You can share your world with everyone, if you want. I'm telling you that everyone can build your world. I see this beauty all around me, and I want to have it, too." He let go of her, shrugging. "This is what he wanted."

She shook her head. "No way. You've always been great at telling me how to spend the little money my father left for me. I just get so sick of hearing about what he would have wanted for me. He wanted me to go to college."

"You're doing that," Chris insisted. "You're doing just fine with that, and there would still be plenty left over. You told me once that you had enough to pay for college more than twice over, so why not make something here that lasts?"

"Yeah, but this is a little robot project. What can my little robot do compared to all of this?"

"I know very little about your little robot, I admit. Talk to Aidan. Find out what it can do, and then see what kind of a world you can build."

They finished dinner and talked about the upcoming month. Caro was thirty days away from submitting her design project, and Chris insisted that a lot could happen in thirty days. As it turned out, school left him swamped, and so most of his encouragement started coming by text messages. He showed up a few days later in a group study room in the library, where she was meeting with her engineering group. He only told her over the phone that he had a big announcement to make. He arrived shortly after with Aidan and Wil in tow, explaining to her that the business students he had been studying with found a space downtown large enough to fit fifty people comfortably, and that they had worked up a full budget that the seniors had already gone over.

"The numbers look realistic," Aidan conceded as they spread out the report on the table surrounded by six chairs. With seven people there, they seemed one chair short except that Wil was too excited to sit as he showed the details from the budget to the group assembled around the table. "Do you really think you can afford all of this?" Caro realized that he was looking straight at her.

"I believe in you, Caro," Chris jumped in. "Even more important, I don't want to limit this beautiful world to just a handful of people. This design project," he fanned his hands out to the pages that now covered the entire table, "is more than just another empty class assignment. You can make it happen, which is why I told them about the money."

"This is too much... how can I possibly explain this much away?" She started to tear up at the thought, and she shook with the magnitude of the project he placed with her. "My mother will freak. There's no way that she would forgive me. I mean, this is what? Twenty grand?"

"You'll finally get to tell your story!" He turned to Aidan and Wil, "Back me up here. Let her know that this is possible. I want everyone to see what I've seen. I know she can do it, because I've seen how much you all enjoy the world she's created."

Aidan ran his hands through his hair. "It's possible, and so much bigger than the boxing game. Do you have any idea what could be accomplished with this? The rest of the groups, they don't have a dime to spend on their projects, or they might spend twenty dollars on cardboard boxes and maybe a new sensor."

"It just sounds crazy, though." Caro tried to process all of it. "Spending such a huge chunk of my inheritance on this? I don't even know if it's fair, considering what everyone else can spend."

Chris laughed as he moved to stand in front of her. "This is not about fairness, and these numbers aren't arbitrary." He gave a knowing glance to Aidan and Wil. "We have talked about this project, in broad numbers mostly. I told them to dream big, and then the business students put everything together to make sure that you wouldn't be resorting to half measures. This business proposal... this is the real deal."

Aidan chimed in, "You can make this dungeon real, and you

won't be alone. Just say the word, and we'll help you turn it into a reality."

Caro considered the responsibility. She never really disliked money, but when it was such a huge amount, it felt too easy to write something off as too extravagant. How could she ever convince herself that she deserved to spend twenty grand on something as un-academic as this big toy that everyone was pitching? "Yes. I mean, I really want to, but only if we can make something truly special. Something worth more than just the sum of the money we're spending on it."

Aidan high-fived Wil and they quickly began making a list of small tasks that the robot could handle. They would have to choose one, but instead of narrowing down, they kept spouting ideas, writing down what they liked most. With their enthusiasm and experience, it didn't take long to get the engineering group on board with the project. The light sensor project was too limited in scope, and they wanted to do something bigger. More importantly, the other three in her engineering group were excited to do something that a group member was passionate about.

Hours later, the study group packed up but Aidan asked Caro to stay behind. "Have you ever done anything like this before?"

"Like what?" Caro twirled her pen in her hand as the weight of the project sat heavier on her. "Drop thousands on something brand new? Invest time, money and stress into something that I have no idea if it's going to work out?"

"Negative Nancy," Aidan laughed. "If you really have the

money to spare, what's keeping you from trying? You keep asking me if we can do it, and I keep telling you yes."

Caro let the thought sink in. The day had been a barrage of ideas, and she felt it all building up to something so much bigger than her and her dad's gift. "I wouldn't say I had the money to spare. The money's there, sure, but I keep thinking that the moment the money is gone, that he'll be gone, too. It sounds crazy, I know."

"Doesn't sound crazy at all." Aidan pulled a chair up to the table, leaning in, "My grandfather left me this chess set, it's all dark and light ivory: gorgeous stuff. The thing is, I don't play. What should it be worth to me? Should I learn to play? Should I sell it for what I can get, maybe buy a car?"

"A car?"

Aidan chuckled. "Yeah. Well, like I said. It's gorgeous. He wanted me to have something nice, and in the end, I think I'll sell it after graduation and buy some antique furniture for my house. It's kind of what he wanted for me, and most of all it's what I want for myself. You say you can build something with this money that your dad would have loved, and you have a group of people that would kill to see your dream come true. Who are you to knock that?"

Caro shrugged, unable to come up with an answer that would let her go back to designing doggy doors.

Late Wednesday night, she crept into her room to find Evie at her computer, working through another photography project. They still hadn't spoken since anime night, except for a brief 'hey'. Backing away from her desk, Evie turned to face Caro.

"This sucks, and I know it's my fault."

Caro didn't disagree, but struggled to think of anything to add to the conversation. "Yeah?"

"Look, I'm sorry, and I can't think of any way to make this up to you just yet, but I will." Evie folded her hands nervously in her lap. "Chad is mad at me."

Caro let out a laugh that was louder than she expected. "No big surprise there."

"He says I stole you from him," she giggled. "He won't shut up about it."

"I don't expect you to fix that. Some things are beyond our control. Things are difficult between us because you never said anything, you just went ahead and did it, and tried to beg forgiveness after. Maybe if you just talked to me first." She still remembered the kiss quite vividly, and blushed when she remembered the feel of soft lips against hers. "Maybe we could have talked it out and you wouldn't have jumped the gun on the whole kissing thing."

"Yeah. I just figured I regret so many more things I haven't done than things I have, you know?"

Caro didn't have a clue, but nodded anyway. "I can put it behind me if you can. I want my roomie back." She held out her arms and gave the best forgiving smile she could muster. "Hug it out?"

Evie hugged her, just a little longer than Caro expected. Clearly, things weren't back to normal. They were still pretty damned awkward, but it was the most she'd talked to her roommate in a week, and she relished having her confidant back. Besides, she wanted to start the game back up, considering that every minute in the fantasy world made her feel better about the engineering project.

"So," Evie nudged, "when can I hear about your date with Chris?"

Caro didn't know where to start with Chris, or where things were going. She figured she was confused enough without input from Evie, and besides, best not to push their luck.

ELEVEN

By the time the rest of the crowd showed up that Tuesday, Chad was already at the table piled behind his character sheet and a row of Mountain Dew. It was a little weird for Caro to think about, because it meant that someone had let him into the girls' dorm and then left him there alone, which was frowned upon in this dorm. She supposed the girls had gotten used to the gamer boys hanging out in the cave and didn't think much of them. Chad really was pretty harmless, and it was good that he hadn't given up the group after he saw anime night as such a betrayal. Ugh. Anime night. The less she thought about it, the better. Still, she felt like an apology might smooth the rough and awkward edges that formed on her favorite close-knit group.

She called to him, and he looked up from his book. "Hey. About last week–"

"Nah, forget it. None of my business." It sounded good on the outside, but Caro wasn't convinced.

You tried to sabotage my date. No, he's none of your business, but how would you know that?

"No, I mean yes. It is in a way. Look." She came in close to sit next to him. "After last week, things are different between us."

"Like, bad different?"

Very bad different, but you can make it up to me by acting like a normal guy.

"No, just different. I guess I never saw you, or Aidan, or," she paused, "well, anyone in that light before last week, and it's all taken me by surprise. I'm sorry if I seemed so quick to push you away, but I really didn't want you to get the wrong idea. I was sure I would have just hurt you more in the long run, and that's the last thing I'd want to do to my friends."

Chad flinched at the f-word, but she pushed through anyway, "I didn't want to give any of my friends the wrong impression, and that's why it's taken most of this week just to be able to talk to Evie again." He scratched at the back of his hand and looked down at the table. She figured he hadn't stayed around for the rest of her conversation with Evie. His upturned eyebrows confirmed it for her. "I'm not interested in anyone in this group that way." She worded herself carefully. "And I want you to know that."

I'm not interested in Evie or you in that way. What is it with gamer boys always going crazy when I try to date outside of the group? And the gamer girl? Well, she was a whole different animal. An amazing animal, but still a resounding no.

"What about your date with Chris?"

Some of her warmth went out of her voice. "Yeah. That one. One day we're going to talk about your dating advice."

You set him up for failure, and he still came out shining like my knight in shining armor was supposed to. Thanks for sealing that deal, but no thanks for trying to act like some kind of mastermind. You're not as smart as you think you are.

Did she see a smirk cross his face? He thought he got away with it. Oh well. If it made things a little more manageable, she figured she'd give him his prank, or sabotage, or whatever he was trying to pull. "Can we move on? The guys I may or may not meet–"

"Or girls." Aidan walked in with Evie and Wil, just in time to get one last remark in before the game started. She held up an arresting finger to him.

"The GUYS I may or may not meet shouldn't have to deal with our past, okay?" She tried to find a better way to say it, because it was starting to feel like they'd dated and then broken up. He seemed to get it, and so she left it where it lay.

The game was a bust before it began. Caro was too far in her own head and wrapped up in the week's events to focus on the game, and things were still weird with half of the people at the table. She needed to do something to get everyone back to normal, so she offered the first thing that came to mind. "Who wants Chinese?"

Rather than try to squeeze in a little Geo Metro with Evie and Chad, Caro went for a less awkward option. She climbed into Wil's beat up old white pickup truck as he jumped into the driver's seat. The beast must have been older than both of them, and it hurtled through traffic like a juggernaut. It swayed with the gentle curves of the road, and watching Wil in the driver's seat of the huge behemoth was like watching a gnome ride a catapult.

They reached an overpass at the edge of campus. Wil leaned over and wondered out the side of his mouth, "The traffic light on the other side of the underpass… green or red?"

"I dunno, red?" Seemed like a safe bet.

"Let's find out," WOOO, she couldn't tell if it was the engine revving or her heart beating like a drum roll, or the screams of one or both of them in the car. They sped through the intersection, barreling under the bridge. They were 30 feet from the light when she finally saw it beaming yellow from under the bottom of the train tracks that ran above the road. Through the muffled cries of her common sense telling her to jump out of the truck because anything would be safer than driving with a madman, she heard his excitement bubbling through his grin, "Neither! Yellow it is."

Caro poured herself out of the aging pickup and into the Chinese restaurant, thankful to be in one piece, unless you count the shattered nerves she'd left somewhere a mile back. The other car hadn't made it yet, so Caro took the time to gather herself. "What the hell was that?"

"Relax," he said. "I've timed it. If I break 50 between the southwest corner light of campus and the start of the school zone, I always make the light." He punched her shoulder for good measure. "I'm just messing with you. Somebody's got to get your head out of the clouds."

It was the first time he talked to her about anything other than magic or engineering. "But you could have killed us! And always? We almost didn't make it!" She was livid. She wanted to survive the school year, and even with all-nighters, crazy hard exams and the social pressures of the awkward, dying in a car accident didn't figure into her plans.

"Okay. Sixty percent of the time." Her jaw dropped and he walked a little closer to her, his long blond hair falling carelessly over his shoulders. He grabbed her by her shoulders, shaking her vigorously. "Relax!"

She laughed as loud as she would allow herself as Evie's car turned into the parking lot. They walked into the restaurant together, Aidan looking suspiciously at Caro. "Riding with Wil? You're braver than I thought."

"No warning? Thanks for setting me up!"

Aidan shook his head. "Not my fault. Everybody's gotta learn."

They found a seat and placed their drink orders. The all-you-can-eat Chinese buffet was one of three, but the only one that anyone with any taste in food went to. The other two restaurants stayed open for years, but how they managed that feat was beyond Caro. She stuffed herself quickly on the first plate, trying to avoid conversation while the crowd settled into their food.

Finally, the group loosened up and they were able to laugh like friends again. They traded game stories, growing up stories, and Caro was trying to figure out in a roundabout way how long Aidan and Evie had been friends. The oldest story she heard either of them tell dated the friendship back to seventh grade. That was the first time Evie set up Aidan with one of the wild girls from her Girl Scout troop. She was pretty sure that she might hear one day that they had been friends for life. She just hadn't gotten that far into the stories just yet.

Evie looked around at the rest of the table joking around and then nodded before motioning for Caro's attention. "I grilled your ex while you were out yesterday."

The smile dropped from Caro's face. "There's a reason why I didn't want to talk about it." The conversation dropped off and Caro and Evie excused themselves to go to the bathroom.

As soon as they returned, Aidan folded his hands and smiled as if to make another sideways comment, but Wil spoke first to break his thought process. "If we can't game, can we at least talk about this dungeon we're building downtown? I mean, how big can we really build it?"

"What's bigger?" She was still working through everything herself. "I want to make it big enough for anyone who wants to play. I want to bring people in who want to swing swords, cast spells…"

"Game master?" Chad finally spoke up.

"Yeah, Chad?"

He backtracked a little. "No, I mean, people could game master. They could bring in their own scenarios. Other people would play their adventures out."

She hadn't considered it. It was one thing to tell her story to the world. It was another leap entirely to create a world where people came to tell their own stories. It was shaping into a realm with infinitely more possibilities. "I like that. That's an awesome thought."

"There's just one problem," Aidan spoke up. "The robot… it's just… there's no way that robot can handle what you're talking about doing."

Caro conceded the point. "This is about more than just a robot. This is… this is the story I've been wanting to tell my whole life. The robot can do something, anything to help me tell that story, right?"

Aidan and Wil exchanged a look. Aidan turned back to Caro, "Now you're thinking like an engineer."

TWELVE

"There you go." Chris' soothing voice acted like an analgesic, working through her foot as the forming bones settled. The paper-white walls of the doctor's office around them made her nervous, but his hands were there to keep her grounded. The old cast was peeled away as tender hands massaged blood back into her leg. Her whole body tingled from the rising sensation. It felt somewhere between a caress and a tickle, and it felt like old times, like the way he used to touch her. He soaked a small sponge and cleaned off some of the plaster from the old cast and dried it as her doctor prepared the soft cast.

Her doctor was a large burly farmer man with a dark ponytail tucked into his scrubs. She had a hard time believing that this guy was a doctor. Everything about him screamed biker, and she was sure that the two could not coexist in the same person. Chris finished drying her foot with a towel as the large man behind him waited, bandages in hand. He cleared his throat, and it wasn't until then that Chris' eyes turned away from Caro. He excused himself as the doctor finished wrapping her foot with the tenderness of a burlap sack.

He gave her strict instructions not to get the soft cast wet, but she'd be free to take it off and reapply it after bathing. "When you need to reapply the cast, you'll have to get more tape." He used his hands to frame her foot and emulate the process of putting on a new cast at home, "Start here, working your way to the–"

"She'll be fine," Chris smiled. "I'll take good care of her."

"Yeah, I bet. Well, if he screws it up, feel free to come back and we'll go through it all again. Damn college kids," he muttered as he signed off on her chart and walked out the doorway. "They think they know everything."

For the first few days, their relationship was better than their high school days ever had been. Chris came by every day bringing food, helping her out of the splint and taking care of her while she worked through her homework assignments in bed. "Please, let me."

That's when he would put his hands on her, and it all felt so natural. Every nerve in her body ached for him to keep moving, keep looking for sore, neglected spots and not to stop until every nerve ending was finished with him. His unbelievable patience seemed to have no end, either. He never stopped before she asked him to, and that was usually only because she felt a nagging pang with her roommate present. When Evie was gone, most of those visits ended with Chris laid up in bed with her, his shoulder pressed into her breast as she held her arm over his other shoulder, fingers playing in his brown, curly hair.

She thought about pushing it further, but nothing felt right about intimacy with him anymore. It was expressly forbidden in the dorms, but then again anything worth doing in the dorms was forbidden. Hot plates, candles, grilling and sex. She was sure there was a long list of things she had no intention of doing in the dorms that was also forbidden. That wasn't what kept her hands off him. The plastic single beds that furnished every room had the feel of an underinflated soccer ball, or a kid's tent filled with wet towels. Lumpy in all the wrong places. That helped, but certainly didn't encompass all of her reasons for not going farther. No agreement was ever struck which specifically allowed her any sort of guarantee of time. Beyond all of this, she tried every day to shake the memory of Evie's kiss and the reminder that she had left her home and Chris behind when she started her new life here.

The following night, he showed up well before dinner and asked her if she had any plans for the evening. When she balked, he gave her the most pitiful look. "Tell me what's going on. Nothing has felt right for days, and I've been trying. What's wrong? Let's get out of this dorm room, get something to eat, listen to loud music, anything. Please come with me."

She couldn't deny that this new Chris was a sight better than the boy she left behind, and she wanted dearly for things to be more than just comfortable, for them to be better. She smiled, hobbling out of bed. "Step out for a second. I'll get ready."

He took her to an aging Italian restaurant on the north side of town where the paint peeled from the brick walls, but everything smelled like garlic and tomatoes. Fake ivy sprouted from every corner, and grapes framed candles on the table. She hadn't seen much of this area of town, even though it was small enough that she should have been to every restaurant within the city limits. The low lights and light music playing over the speakers were lovely. When the food came, the delicious flavors blended into each other and she lost herself in the meal. Chris barely ate. He sat next to her with a hand in her lap, drawing small circles on her knee that echoed across the rest of her body. She felt worshipped.

"You followed me, even after everything I said back home. I barely give you the time of day here, when we have time to visit, and even then you know that things have changed. Why do you still try so hard?" She shook her head at his stubbornness. "What's so special about me?"

Chris cleared his throat, taken aback. "You think you're not special?" She shook her head, shooting him a disbelieving look. "You have showed me your world. Let me show you what I see. Close your eyes."

In the darkness, a beating heart shone out from a crowd of lifeless paper people. "Do you really think you aren't special?" It beat slightly faster, sending life out among the paper people. One by one, the paper people came to life. "This is the first thing I see when I see you. I see you breathing life into the world, one person at a time. If it had just been me, that would be one thing, but I see what you do for all of us."

Slowly, the beating heart breathed life into the rest of the crowd, each undulating in the same lifeblood. The heart formed into a brain, neural pathways stretching out until the small organ that looked like a labyrinth of gray matter spread out into miles of highway, leading to hundreds of beautiful locations.

"Oh, I see. You just like me for my brains?" She felt like she was fishing. She hated that, but she wanted him to keep talking. She wanted him to say something that would spark the fire that she used to carry for him.

"Oh, that's the bonus. I assure you." Chris pulled his arm up and around her, lying over the far shoulder and barely brushing her breast from the other side. Her heart skipped a beat as he pulled her close. "The bonus that outshines the rest." He kissed her deeply. The restaurant tipped on its axis and she dropped her hands from his chin, knocking the plate of spaghetti in front of her onto their laps.

Chris tried not to laugh. She sat mortified, wondering how best not to draw attention to herself. She picked up the plate from her lap, leaving the spaghetti where it lay out in an intricate pattern across the crotch of her red skirt. She supposed that was the best blessing in disguise. What happened if spaghetti stains didn't get out of red clothing?

He walked her back to her dorm in an awkward silence. Things had changed. Of course, he had changed for her and done everything she could ever have asked him to do. In the short time they were apart, the things that she wanted most had shifted too far for him to follow. It was still before ten when she walked through her door, but Evie was in bed already. Caro had seen her in this morose mood before when the stress of exams weighed heavily on her. What used to cheer her up best, before all the complications at anime night, was the chance to sit and talk with cartoons playing in the background, or when Caro would just eat while Evie bitched about art professors and their impossibly finicky grading methods. She rather enjoyed those nights.

Chris lingered at the door before Caro held a hand up to usher him out. "It's been fun, but I think we should call it a night–"

"I understand." Chris nodded sheepishly, and Caro wasn't sure he really did until he saw her roommate lying in bed. "So sorry, Evie. Good night." He walked himself out and the thought of escorting him out the building barely came to mind as Caro looked at Evie. She was awake now, though Caro couldn't have been sure how alert she was, or how much of it truly was the result of a bad day of classes.

"Sorry if I woke you." Caro sat on her bed a few feet away from Evie, her knees pointed in and eyeing the new stain on her red skirt. "We ate at this Italian restaurant. I got spaghetti sauce all over my lap. It was terrible." She hoped to draw some sort of reaction. Evie blinked a little, taking in the scene and then turning over in her bed.

"I'll just let you rest." Caro's voice quieted as she took off her shoes. When she reached to turn out the light, she saw Evie's shoulder's shaking from under the covers and immediately reached in to comfort her. "Hey... hey..."

Evie didn't turn around. The sobs increased a little when Caro touched her, so Caro did the only thing she thought she could do. She kneeled down on the floor next to Evie's bed and laid her arm and head over on her roommate. It was awkward. The position on the floor hurt her knees, and she couldn't get the kiss out of her head. She held her half embrace as long as she could, and within a few minutes, the sobbing slowed.

"I don't know what's going on. I can't even pretend to have kept up with things in the past few weeks. I'm here to talk if you ever need to, and sometimes I can just be here for a hug if you need it."

She lowered herself back to sit on her feet from the kneeling position and Evie let out a long sigh. All of the shaking gone from her shoulders, she reached a hand up and over to hold Caro's hand on top of her arm. They sat like that for a while until Caro got uncomfortable and moved up into bed, wrapping up Evie in her arms and going to sleep in silence. She tried to be a comfort, but the relief that felt so much like home lulled her into quick, deep sleep.

THIRTEEN

JuJu, Lars and Patrick sat around a table in the library. Caro drew up several possibilities, but Lars didn't seem so sure. "All I'm saying is, it seems a little bit late. 20 days to turn in a project, and we're switching it up? Why can't we just keep the old project? We'll pass."

"Ugh. Forget passing." Caro was fired up, excited to get them on board. She hadn't expected resistance from the guy who put in so little effort. "Look, just think of it this way: We'll do everything. It's not like you were going to work on it."

"Hey. I would have. No one ever gives me anything to do."

Caro tried to remember the last time they'd given him an assignment. He was the invisible man. He never showed up, so why would they ask him to bring anything to the next class, or research anything for them? "Do you want something to do?" He shrugged, and that was the end of their disagreement.

"We can do it. It's not an impossible deadline, but what makes this project so special? Will it be all that much better than our previous one?" Patrick spoke up. Caro figured that was all she needed to get him on board. Obviously she piqued his interest enough to get him involved verbally.

"The light sensor that turns plants toward the sun was a solid idea," Caro offered, "but who's going to buy it? We can make it work, we can prove that there's a need, but there's no way anyone will pay money for a product that moves plants four times a day. What kind of a market share would we have?" She just started using words she'd vaguely picked up from some business students in the cafeteria.

"And, you think the gamers are a better market?" JuJu wasn't entirely convinced, but she smiled at seeing someone, anyone fired up about making something that mattered to them.

"Gamers will follow. Gamers vote with their money. That's how the hobby shops have managed to stay open. That's how comic books get sold. That's why you see card collecting games in Walmart and Walgreens." She was getting their attention. Now she had to tell them the bad news. "Our little robot won't do it all, though." She pulled out the robot and put it on the table. "Its memory will hold only a little bit of code. It can run through several lines of code, even, but once that code is in there, that's it. We can give it a handful of things to do, maybe three, and then we've reached its limit."

"So, we can only do half of a project?" Patrick seemed ready to get up from the table. It was time to call in the big dogs.

Aidan walked up to them with a softcover book and a little maroon binder. "We can do it all. You can do enough to make a good impression on the engineering faculty."

Aidan laid out the big plan as best as he could. He spent the majority of the night up, looking through code books, code snippets, and the latest research journals on instrumentation and database coding. While he admitted there was little that the fifty dollar robot they used in class could handle, the rest of the project would be powered by state-of-the-art sensors and modeling programs. The Living Dungeon would have generic silhouettes of monsters with LCD screens that would change colors and display a face on top of its shoulders. They would use RFID and databases to track the statistics of every hero, game master and monster in the room, and they would have a combat system based closely on game rules that Caro and her game group used to keep the AI simple enough to put into the program.

"So, it looks like you've got all this figured out. What do you need us for?" Juneau crossed her arms. "Looks like the seniors already have all of this planned out."

Aidan pulled a small wooden dagger from his backpack. He leveled it at her eyes, "I challenge you, Lady Juneau, to tell the beast when it is dead."

Caro jumped up from the library table, gesturing with her hands in her excitement, jumping on the bandwagon where the interest was sparked. "It's simple, really. The problem that our group will be tasked with will be a simple customer-engineer issue. The monsters' LCD bodies, LED screens and databases need to interface with each other. We need to use the information in the database to turn off lights, change the picture on the LCD screen and list the monster as dead."

Lars finally appeared to perk up. He had nearly been napping, lulled to sleep by apathy. The idea of something dying woke him, "So, why are we killing monsters again? I don't get it."

Juneau seemed confused, too. Patrick just looked on with a

blank stare, pretending to follow but without an answer for Lars.

Caro took a deep breath. It was one thing to explain to the gamers who had elves in their computer games to shoot at the orcs. Anyone who followed Tolkien could catch up pretty quickly in other medieval fantasy games. She started them off as slowly as she could.

She circled the table and laid out a dirt path leading up to a campfire in a lush forest. Six stones surrounded the licking flames, each one big enough to seat the travelers.

Juneau kicked the rock. "Is this real?"

"Real enough." Caro brought in a small, fair skinned gnome. His pointy ears made the lines in his clothing sharper. He barely reached waist height on any of them. With a swift jig, he jumped into the campfire, kicking burning logs around him to make the flames dance.

"I need to sit down." Lars didn't seem to be handling the changing scenery as well as the others. "I think my brownies are kicking in."

"Don't be silly," Caro encouraged him. "The game isn't a drug or a place. The game is a way to relax, to get away from..." she tried not to talk too harshly about her own company, "libraries, or—"

"Kids." Patrick looked at the dirt trails leading into the campfire, and then walked over to the gnome. Shaking hands, the gnome mumbled incoherently and squeaked out a few sounds. "He rubbed his own fingers together after the handshake, wiping the soot of the fire off of them. "His skin is... soft, cool to the touch."

"He's immune to fire. That's Flamebreaker. He's a favorite of mine." Caro raised her eyebrows as the skies darkened. "He's especially good with daggers."

A swift wind picked up, scattering the logs to smoldering cinders and ash. Flamebreaker ducked his head low and perked his ears. The wind rushing through the trees perked senses up within him and he let out a small growl.

"These woods aren't safe." Caro grinned. "What would you do if you wanted to survive, say, a Ranger Assassin?"

Black bolts soared into the encampment in the twilight. Flamebreaker rolled and pulled out his twin daggers, coating his hands in ice. The blue blades sung with the wind around him as he peered into the deep darkness of the forests. More bolts flew at his feet as he ran for the wooded edge of the encampment.

"Aaahh, I QUIT I QUIT I QUIT!" The library seemed to quake with the sudden jolt back to reality. Lars got slowly up from the table and looked to Caro. "Is it safe? I've had some bad trips before, but this–"

"This is beautiful." Patrick sat slowly back into his chair. "It's like getting lost in a book, but for the whole group." He started to sketch on a notepad in front of him. His mouth moved with intensity as he made bold, sweeping arcs across the page. Caro wasn't quite sure where he was going with this.

"Let's say I was on a submarine in the Pacific Ocean, just waiting for some sign that a war was starting." He continued to sketch computer desks, a periscope, and handful of people. "Let's say the guy next to the crazy red button that launches a nuclear missile found a way to steal the launch codes, but needed to enlist the help of the XO, trying to gauge how best to turn a loyal leader into a defector…" The scenarios played its way through his head. He was getting a good feel for the suspense, fun and excitement of drastic situations. Caro hadn't considered putting in options for the game for modern settings, but if he contributed more there, maybe he'd get more excited.

"Yeah, sure. I can see how you might look at it that way." Caro hadn't pictured the game being used this way. "I mean, sure. It's not just dragons and wizards. It's any situation you can put a character of yours in, and then ask yourself how they'd act."

Aidan jumped in. "So, this new world that we're proposing, the Living Dungeon, is a small room downtown where we've started setting everything up." Aidan explained.

Wil tossed mind maps on the table with scenarios webbing out across ten pages. "We should be able to get the dummy with software for these scenarios loaded to you in a week. That gives you a week to come up with the program, and another two weeks to make it work."

Patrick flipped through the scenarios as he worked through a mental list, "I think I have a few ideas how we can make this happen." He looked up to Caro. "This is good stuff, kid. Here I thought I'd never be asked a question I genuinely looked forward to answering in this class."

JuJu bit on a pencil. "Aidan, can you forward some documentation on these sensors to me? I'll look through the communication protocols on the equipment you've got. If you can give me a spec sheet printout, I can possibly get some work done on it today." Her hands shook with excitement. "And Caro... do you think I could go back to the campfire one day?"

"I tried lighting a campfire once." Lars sat motionless, staring straight ahead where the fire was. "Caught my pants on fire."

"Lars." He didn't budge. "Hey." Caro snapped her fingers and moved to get into his line of vision. "Why are you even here?" When he wouldn't answer, she tried to spur him into... something. Action? Motivation? Leaving? "You want to waste your time, you've got one week for it. Once we have all the equipment here, though, I'll need you to come up with the artwork."

"Why me?" It was the first request they'd given him. He was shocked.

"Because this is MY dream, and if you want to put your name on it, you'll have to put a hand on it."

Juneau packed up quietly, then walked off with Aidan while she asked questions about the sensors he'd found. Patrick and Wil talked excitedly as they headed out, with Patrick making up modern scenarios and Wil comparing them to fantasy themes.

"I'm sorry." Caro sat next to Lars and looked him in the eyes for the first time since she snapped at him. "I wasn't trying to say that you're not helpful."

"I get it," he shrugged. "Nobody ever counts on me. When they do, I just let them down." Lars drew his eyes to the table and the engineering notes in front of him. Caro looked for some way to make it better. She wasn't sure what sparked the sudden change in his demeanor. She was even less sure that there was anything she could say to make it right, when she had been the one to make him so morose. As she packed up her notes, she walked away and left him to his thoughts. With the rest of the table gone, his countenance steeled. He pulled blank paper from his notebooks and started scribbling equations furiously onto the page.

FoURTEEN

A bright white light flashed in the dark room where Caro leaned against Chris in front of the big screen television. They had been lucky to get the dorm common area to themselves on such a nice Sunday afternoon. The movie was one of his favorites, but Caro wasn't watching. She could feel his breath on her neck. He hadn't done anything differently, and maybe that's why she had let this go on as long as it had.

She shifted uncomfortably and checked her phone. Her mother had been texting her on and off for the past two weeks about withdrawals from her bank account. She was already trying to work through so much. All she pictured was her mother's overbearing tone and criticism. She muted the phone, and Chris looked over her shoulder. "You know," he started, "you should call her." She turned the phone off and stared at the pale walls. "She worries about you. We all do."

The music on the TV swelled and she could feel his eyes on the back of her head. He brushed his hands on her shoulder. "She called me the other day. She said she was worried about all this money that you're spending now. She says you're going to go through it too quickly, that you'll get in over your head and not be able to finish college. I set her straight. I told her that you had a good group of guys up here helping you through it. I told her that you know what you're doing."

She exhaled, short and quick. She stared at the blank screen on her phone fully expecting that her mouth would tell him goodnight, but her staggered voice mumbled meekly. "There's someone else." She saw images for the first time on the TV. Two guys were dueling it out with swords, fighting over some obnoxiously gorgeous girl. They started singing and she tried to figure out how she got suckered into watching a musical. Just as the dastardly duke swished his sword through high notes, her stomach growled.

"Who is it? Was it something I did? Talk to me."

"You've gotta go. It's time for supper." She crossed her arms and tried to appear resolute without looking back. She would be looking forward to comfort food. She needed something warm and bad for her. Grilled cheese and tomato soup were always good for that. Maybe she'd luck out in the cafeteria. She needed time and greasy sandwiches and Evie. She needed the most solid rock in this small town. Evie was the only thing that could keep her from washing out to sea now that Chris' ship was sailing.

She excused herself and ushered him out of the building before heading back to the dorm. Evie was engrossed in a Japanese cartoon, headphones on and sitting too close to her computer screen. Caro walked over to Evie's chair and stood by her. As Evie finally looked up, oblivious to her surroundings, she turned her chair to face Caro. Caro brought a leg over in front of the chair, and sat down sideways in Evie's lap, wrapping up in her arms. The headphone cord stretched, pulling almost completely off of Evie's ears as she tried to process everything.

"Um… tough day?"

"Boys suck."

"Got it." Evie wrapped her arms around Caro, working her body so that the two of them fit together like jigsaw puzzles. Caro's big sweater felt like being wrapped up in covers, and Evie took a moment just to sit and enjoy the moment while her heart broke for her good friend. For the second time that afternoon, Caro's stomach growled.

Caro gave the best pout she could muster. "I want grilled cheese. Cafeteria run?"

"It's worth a shot," Evie said, and then began to stutter through her thoughts. "Um, but I'm not quite ready. Can I meet you there?"

Caro stood and grabbed her purse. She didn't know why she expected Evie to be more comforting, but she supposed she'd done everything a roommate could do. Trying not to sulk, she asked on her way out the door, "See you there in 10?" Evie nodded and Caro walked out the door. She turned on her phone and was greeted with a constant nagging buzzing at missed calls and messages.

"Mom, I'm fine."

"You don't seem fine. Honey, what have I told you about not keeping in touch? I was about to call in the National Guard."

Caro rubbed her arm against the chill with her free hand as she picked up the pace. "Would you relax?"

"We need to talk about all of this money. Chris tells me you're relying on a student business plan. That doesn't sound like the little genius I raised." Caro figured only her mother could make the word 'genius' sound so derisive. "I want to hear more about this… thing you're spending all your father's money on."

"You'll see it when it's finished, I promise." Caro dreaded showing her mother a half-finished product, but wondered how much longer she could stall. "Do you trust me?"

"It's not about whether I trust you." Somehow Caro seriously doubted her mother's assertion. "I just want to make sure you're covering all of your bases."

Caro kept moving toward grilled cheese. She let the silence hang in the air.

"Is what Chris saying true? Is it really what your father would have wanted?"

"I know it is," she lied. Caro would sit in her dream world once a week now to visit with the ghost of her father, but she was sure that the more he assured her, the more her subconscious had taken over trying to allay her fears about the significant investment.

"I guess that's all that matters, then."

The remainder of the short walk to the cafeteria would have been nicer in warmer weather. On warmer days, she enjoyed walking past the dogwood trees and taking in the colors that speckled the college campus, both from the flowering bushes and trees as well as the diversity of students from all over the globe that came to this empty town just to graduate from Northeastern University. Her boots clicked against the cold concrete and she tried to look up only enough to keep from running into the people that passed by. The chill made it easier to bundle herself up and not have to smile at everyone. It was nice living in a state where everyone you make eye contact with gives you a smile and a friendly wave, but some days she just wanted to ignore them all.

Today she did, damn polite southern society.

Grilled cheese was there, but vegetable soup would have to satisfy her tomato soup craving. She found a table in the back corner, even though coming early to dinner meant there weren't many people to avoid. She picked at her food for a few minutes until she saw Evie come in the door with a backpack. She figured Evie hadn't been able to finish what was so important, but then again she didn't expect much. Skipping the meal line, Evie came over to the table and put her backpack down on the other side, out of view.

"Alright, girl. Get'em up." Evie gestured to clear the table as she pulled a white sheet into view. Caro shrugged, then tried to follow the setup. In a matter of minutes, Evie put up a white table cloth, a scented candle and two wine glasses on the table.

"What's this?"

"Sounds like Loverboy botched your Sunday date. I figured you could use a fancy meal." Evie smiled and moved to Caro's side of the table, hopping into a chair beside her. She paused for a second, surveying her work, "Does this count? I can totally go back and get an apron. I'm a kickass waitress."

"No," Caro laughed to herself. "This is perfect." She couldn't picture anything but the table setting. She hadn't even thought of her miserable revelation since Evie's surprise. She couldn't think of a better remedy. Then the word rang in her ears again, "Is this a date?"

"Sure," Evie insisted. "It's a makeup date. I figure you deserve it."

"I don't... I–"

"Okay. Date is a four letter word. I won't bring it up again, except…" Evie twirled a small silver ring on her finger. "It's not a four-letter word where I come from." She held it out for inspection, "This ring was a gift. My dad gave it to me. He used to take me on these amazing Daddy-Daughter dates. We used to go to seafood restaurants, and he would always tell me to get whatever I want." She sat on her hands, bouncing around like a child as she recalled it. "We all went on dates, me and my sisters. He would take us on our own days, and we'd get to spend an afternoon with him all to ourselves."

They talked over grilled cheese. Caro finally put a year on Evie and Aidan's friendship. They met when they were both nine and in band. Aidan was the only boy willing to play the flute, and Evie was the only girl that would talk to a boy that played the flute. From there, things just naturally progressed into the kind of deep friendship that made intimacy just weird for her. "I never knew what to think of him when I started looking at boys. It's not like he's not cute, but he passed over into this weird place where you try to describe someone and the only word that fits is their name. Other girls asked why I never dated him and all I could say was, 'Oh, that's just… Aidan."

"You friend-zoned him?" Caro wasn't eating her sandwich anymore. She made little smiley faces with the grease from the bread on the tablecloth.

"There was no such thing as friend-zones at that age. Just boys you might date and boys that you wouldn't. I didn't see anything wrong with hanging out with him and not dating him, and he never seemed all that interested in me." She shrugged, "Aidan's never been interested in dating anybody, as crazy as that sounds. He's the world's most chaste pervert."

Caro had to agree. From what she'd seen of their time together, Chad was always chasing something. Lately that had been her. Wil would occasionally bring up the same name over and over again until Caro was sure she had been some great love of his life he'd never fully recovered from. Evie, well. Evie had been obvious enough lately about whom she was interested. Caro let that thought sink in while she looked at the nice table arrangement, the soda poured into the wine glasses and the soup bowls on the grease-smeared table cloth.

"This is a real date. This isn't just some silly attempt to get me to feel better about Chris." She looked at the girl across the table from her. Caro had her own ideas about how dates should go, her ideal type, which she admitted was normally male, and her expectations of how things should go physically on a date. Evie didn't match any of those expectations, but had managed to exceed them on a completely different level that Caro hadn't expected. The gesture was kind, and it was exactly what she needed.

Caro couldn't deny that there was something different about Evie today. Something shifted when Caro told her that she needed her. She tried to imagine that this was what she always tried to act like. She tried to imagine Evie always dropping some subtle hint about the way she wanted things to be. "Things have changed. I didn't want them to, but they have."

Evie couldn't argue with that. She leaned against Caro and

whispered, "You can't move to a brand new place, make all new friends, and work through all of this pressure without changing. I don't blame you."

Caro jolted. "Me? How have I changed?"

"I don't know. I remember this quiet, scared girl that showed up in my dorm room a few months ago. Now I see this girl who's on top of the world, making stuff she never would have dreamed of making when she came here."

Caro thought about the dungeon, and all of her big plans for it. It seemed a world away from the journal she brought with her. She fondly remembered Chris. Their time together was good but over, she decided. She thought about being a game master for the first time ever, and carrying on the legacy that her father inspired within her. This wasn't the girl she saw in the mirror, but she liked that someone saw it. She recalled the real date with Chris that started to feel fake the more she drifted. She relished how much more 'real' it felt to be with Evie. "This was nice. Thank you."

Evie shrugged. She grabbed her hand, not even pretending to eat the mediocre food in front of them. She leaned in and rested her head on Caro's shoulder.

FIFTEEN

"Are you sure? I know it means so much to you," Caro looked at the small silver ring that Evie slipped on her finger. Evie's hands were so much bigger than hers that she was able to slide it over her thumb and twirl it nervously. "It was your dad's after all."

"He gave it to me on our Daddy-Daughter date, so it seems only right that I give this to you to wear tonight. Now, get ready so we can get out of here!"

There was something weird about getting dressed in the room now. Caro never felt awkward before. She felt strange changing in front of Evie, but not weird enough to say anything. More to the point, she got this tingling in her gut that wouldn't go away, and she didn't want it to. She went through her closet. She still hadn't washed her favorite dress from date night, so she settled for a green dress that was more muted under the night lights. They were going to a club, and the last thing she wanted was to dress in sequins and feel like the disco ball. She only wanted one person with their eyes on her, and she was already in the room, changing too.

Caro pulled off her shirt and became more aware of her nakedness than usual. She hadn't changed with Evie in the room since anime night, and she didn't want to bring up the awkwardness that stood between them in the days following it. Instead, she zipped up her green dress, looking behind her to see if Evie was looking. Evie was down to a pair of white cotton panties and a tan bra. Rather than look away, Caro let her imagination drift, seeing her the way she sometimes imagined men. The curve under her butt was more defined than a man's, drawing a light shadow underneath it. The curves of her waist sloped in, which was a long way from the masculine inverted triangle. Evie grabbed a white and black dress from her closet and turned to put it on. When she turned toward the door, she saw Caro looking at her.

Busted. She didn't turn away, though. She walked toward her instead, handing her the dress. "A little help here?" Caro took the dress from her and opened it up at her ankles. When Evie stepped in, Caro pulled it up, putting her arms in and stopping along the way to admire curves in a way she never pictured before. As she zipped up the dress, she remembered being envious of girls' bodies in the past. She never wanted one before tonight.

"Do we really have to do this?" Caro half begged, knowing how weird it might get.

"Yes. The boys need to get off campus, and I can't think of anywhere funnier I'd like to take them." It was Evie's idea to go to the club. Caro hadn't pictured herself inside a club, though she was sure it wouldn't be far removed from her old dances. The last dance she remembered was in middle school. Middle school dances were horribly awkward because the boys lined along the walls and handed out scores for the girls that danced. She felt like a four out of ten then, as today. The boys that left the comfort of the wall to dance always danced way too close after puberty kicked in, and by that time dances started to feel like a football game with less padding and more grabbing.

Finally all dolled up, Caro held Evie by the hand before walking out the door with one last plea, "Last chance to stay in and play video games."

"In due time." Evie took Caro by the chin and gave her second kiss, deep and slow before nudging her out the door.

After all the time they'd spent putting on dresses, makeup, and Evie straightening her hair, they saw the boys walking over to meet them in jeans and t-shirts. "Aw, come on, you guys. I know you can do better than that." Caro figured if she must get dolled up, the boys could at least put something on with buttons.

Chad looked down at his black jeans and Metallica shirt. "This is a classic band! What's wrong with wearing something I love?" Aidan hadn't tried much harder, but at least his shirt didn't have writing on it. Wil wore what Caro assumed was the only pair of blue jeans he owned and a black shirt with white writing on it that said WILL CODE FOR SEX.

Evie convinced Caro that this was the most they were going to get out of them, and that they were joining the girls at the club, and that was what mattered most. Wil offered to drive, but everyone said "No" in astounding unison. They piled out of Evie's crossover vehicle and into the parking lot of The Blue Rose. The faint but unmistakable WUB WUB of the electronic music drifted among the vehicles. It was eleven already, but Evie insisted that no self-respecting party crasher would arrive a minute earlier. Aidan agreed, adding that they fit well within the group that could have arrived as early as they wanted.

In the darkness of the club, the boys took a hard left past the door when they saw a group of tables near the bar. "No, no." Evie insisted. "You boys are always bitching about not meeting girls. You're not hanging out at a table all night. That's what our Tuesdays are for." She pushed them from behind, moving their way into the center of the dance floor. The club was a flashing mix of light, sound, and sweat. Groups of girls interspersed among the coupled crowd, wooing over drinks and bouncing to the rhythm of the bass. Chad turned to walk toward one group, but quickly retreated back to Aidan and Wil.

"Ugh. I'm not doing all the work tonight. Here…" Evie danced through the crowd, snaking arm in arm with the three boys toward Chad's point of interest. The three girls sipped tall green drinks with neon straws. They definitely weren't a fan of whiskey. As Evie bounced to the music, growing more emphatic with every step, the girls joined in and laughed at her infectious smiling. Before long, the three boys and five girls were lost in the music, swaying in the sea of bodies.

Aidan did his best to copy the guys around him. His blond hair slapping his forehead as sweat beaded on his skin. Wil bobbed his head from side to side, his long hair whooshing through the air. Chad found his own beat, holding his feet out a little over shoulder length and thrusting one fist in the air, banging his head and threatening to pierce his chin on the sharp letters of his Metallica t-shirt.

Evie slid out from the crowd to join Caro leaning against a wall. Sweat made her white dress cling to her, and she was out of breath from the music and the excitement. The bass thudded against their chests. Evie yelled something at her, but neither could hear anything.

Caro tried to shake away the pounding of the bass that beat into her head and chest, and she found a refuge at a small cluster of tables away from the speakers focused on the dance floor. Evie followed her away from the dance floor where they were able to hear a little bit better.

Caro pulled her hair back, taking in everything around them. "This is insane."

"I know, right?" Mumble mumble mumble. Caro leaned in closer, so Evie repeated herself, "I use to go out dancing all the time. There wasn't much else worth doing on the weekends."

"And?"

"And nothing. Moved out here and just haven't had anyone to go out with. I'm not going out by myself!"

Caro pictured the life of a party girl and what it might be like to go out every night, surrounded by all the noise and desperate people. Guys with slicked back hair chatted up girls dressed like blow up dolls. Guys grinded against girls who clinked beers with friends. Nothing looked appealing to her. Was this what Evie needed? "Um, how about once a month?" She figured she could survive one assault on her eardrums for a few hours each month.

Evie looked around, bewildered. "Here? No way! I've got something much better!"

The music melted away into an indiscernible rumbling from the ground beneath them, resonating in their chests. Sticky hardwood floors shifted into dark porous rock and the heat of hundreds of bodies shifted into the wavy intensity of magma pouring out from the cracks of a massive volcanic formation beneath them. Magma floated up as the rumbling of the volcano set the ground on fire. She grabbed Caro by the hand. "I hate this small town drama, and sometimes even getting lost in the music isn't enough. When I really need to get away, I always go back to an old vacation where I was happiest. After all, what's more adventurous than a volcano?" A bubble of lava burst, spraying slag in the air a short distance away. They walked closer to the rim of the volcano. Balanced precariously on the lip, Evie pulled Caro up to meet her and they gazed into the waves of molten rock in the pit below.

"Do you trust me? Because this is going to be awesome." The temptation pulled at her, nudging her to the edge. Evie pulled Caro close until they were both teetering over the edge, Evie dancing against her and holding both of her hands. The waves rocked to their rhythm, and Caro felt the ground falling out from beneath her.

The speaker rocked beneath them as they fell into the waves of people, holding them up and carrying them across the sea of hands. The sound waves pushed through them, carrying them through the flow. Caro was burning up, consumed by the heat and the vibrations. Her heart beat out of control, and her body rocked into Evie's when the crowd finally set them down. She grabbed Evie and pulled her close, kissing her hard. The crowd roared, swaying to the heavy bass. Evie grabbed her by the hand and stopped dead. "The ring!"

A deep pit formed in Caro's stomach, compounded by the twisting agony on Evie's face. They turned back into the crowd, parting those partiers who could be moved to accommodate them. The flashing lights made searching the dance floor nearly impossible. Beer bottles and napkins mushed together into a toxic black hole of alcohol and cherry stems. Caro felt tossed about in the waves of people and bad decisions, searching through the trampling feet felt like wading through dark and heavy waters. They frantically pulled people aside that would listen, motioning to them to tell them about a ring. The few that heard shrugged and swayed to the beat.

The music stopped an hour later and the lights went up. The bartender, manager and door man all insisted that they would let her know if they found anything, but Caro felt as if she had tossed the ring into Mount Doom, never to return. They looked through all the cups and bottles and on all the tables. Chad, Wil and Aidan joined in the effort, even looking along all of the baseboards and helping to pick up all the beer-soaked napkins in hopes of catching the ring before it was thrown away.

Caro was standing by the door, barely able to meet Evie's eyes. Evie smiled weakly, "It's just stuff. We should probably get back."

The five of them piled into the car and drove back in silence while Caro relived the frantic search for the ring over and over again.

SIXTEEN

"Alright, kids. Gather round!" Caro absolutely loved carrying the robot on a dolly into the library. She was finally adjusting to the idea of spending thousands of dollars every day to get things set up in the dungeon downtown. Unpacking the robot had been a labor of love, as she pored over the installation instructions and connected the processor boards to the back where they would be working with all of their inputs and outputs. The whole thing took up the entire size of the four-foot red dolly, and it weighed barely over a hundred pounds even though much of it was rivets and steel frame.

She turned the input board toward them, going over the points and trying to guess where each one should go. Aidan declined to attend, and that nibbled away at Caro's confidence. She always felt more comfortable around electronics with the studied gravity that Aidan brought to everything silicon. Aidan and Wil had been at the dungeon downtown for much of the night before and most of today getting terrain in place and setting up sensors for the grid that the visitors would walk on. Caro always assumed it would take a lifetime of coding to put together the dungeon, but she was amazed at what Wil had been able to come up with through sample codes they pulled from people all around the world trying to build their static dungeons.

While they had never been called that before, the gaming crew felt like they needed to name their competition if there would be any way of differentiating themselves from them. The code that Wil had been able to find became heavily modified, then, as they came up with a system run on an iPad that would allow the first guest to put together the scenario from a list of possibilities, or to do more by creating challenges from scratch. All in all, the 6 monster bodies, dozen obstacles on the ground, scores of grid squares for walking and weapons for monsters and visitors alike already pushed them within ten thousand dollars from their original budget. She was amazed at how good money could put together such an amazing room.

Instead of playing with the boys, though, she was in the library working through the code that would, she hoped, pass her on to her next engineering class and cement her role as innovator on a team that otherwise just pulled together resources and made it work for their own goals. She would have to work twice as hard with her small team to make their engineering robot make all the decisions on the death of the monster.

She shuddered to think about everything that needed to be done. She came up with a list of tasks, subroutines and classes that would have to be assigned in order to issue the final output from the robot, which they aptly named the Death Certificate. Rather than trying to tackle everything today, she worked out a chart of things that needed to be done inside the code, tested, then implemented into the final code. Patrick made the suggestion that nothing that doesn't work would be put into code longer than a dozen lines, so that meant little projects that could often be tackled in just fifteen minutes, but their backtracking would always be on the same scale.

They broke off into little groups with the coding, and Caro stared at the blinking cursor and waited for a word to come. Her mind blanked and she looked down at the keys. Words didn't form right away, so she forced a few. Three words in, she backspaced, started over, deleted again. Everything looked ridiculous on the screen, and nothing was popping into her head. Writer's block was one thing when she just needed to get the players into the tavern to meet the other characters. With this, she just sat, waiting for some line of code to present itself, willing it to jump onto the computer screen.

She started from the middle. She knew the command she needed to get to. From there, she developed a name for a subroutine and then jumped to another section where she worked it out. Going back to her woefully short lines of code at the top, she started mentally working her way back to the front.

Patrick sped through the first routine written under his name before packing his laptop in his bag. "Sorry guys. The kids need me, and their mom can't get off work. I'll do what I can tonight if I can sit them in front of a movie or something." Caro was putting the finishing touches on her section as he was getting up to leave. She was relieved that even if he was getting more unreliable, he was fast with the time that he allotted to his assigned sections.

She peeked over to Juneau's computer screen. She began

testing her small routine, and everything looked like it was progressing well. Caro wondered why it felt like she was the only person who was pulling her hair out. Then she wondered if the rest of the group got the talk about making the project count if they wanted to succeed. Hell, even Lars seemed extremely relaxed. Well, maybe a bit too relaxed.

Caro got up and walked around the table to Lars. When she rounded the corner, she saw a black screen with white pixels rushing across it.

"Seriously, Lars? Space invaders?"

"What?" He pulled his headphones down and looked at the other two at the table. "Did we start?" A faint smell wafted over to her from Lars. He showed up high. Why the hell did he show up high?

She slammed his laptop shut as she slid the papers strewn about the table to him. "You're unbelievable, you know that? We've got two weeks to do this, and you can't even focus on the first day of programming because you're stoned?"

"Nah, it's not like that. It helps me think."

Caro was livid. Her face was heating up and she just kept picturing spending the rest of her life homeless, jobless, hopeless. "Jesus, Lars."

The heat faded from her cheeks and she realized that Juneau was trying to shrink into her seat. Caro had never felt this much rage before. She didn't like what school was doing to her. She wanted to be the easy-going one, the one with the great stories, and the one that people escape to.

Right now, all she wanted to do was escape away from the project. The programming language, which was very similar to the ubiquitous C++ had been a pain already, but now that she started debugging the program something went wrong. It wouldn't compile, and everything she did seemed to only make it worse. A fix on line 11 became a problem on line 12. Everything she did just seemed to make the debug go into spasms and spit the code back out. It took her nearly an hour to write her short code, and even that felt like miserable failure. It could take three hours to sort through it all line by line, comma by comma.

Meanwhile, Evie and Caro spent most nights huddled around Japanese cartoons, snuggled up as the random storylines, ninjas and zombies and explosions flickered across the screen. It wasn't a sappy love story, but she supposed that she liked that it was different. This budding... thing was more than just a friendship, but it was nowhere as hot or intense as things with Chris had been. Aside from small stolen kisses, not much happened. Caro was still getting used to the idea of lip gloss and girly scents that struck her as beautiful. She didn't want to push it any faster than it needed to be pushed.

Two days later, they were back in the library working together as she shook off her distractions and sat back down in front of the blinking red code. "I don't get it." Juneau looked over at the error messages and cringed. She tried to think about what Wil would do. Could he do it? Could he swoop in and save the day?

She slumped at her chair and threw her hands to her sides. She couldn't ask him for this one. He was the expert, sure, but this wasn't the dungeon downtown. This was the final engineering project. There just wasn't any way that she felt it would be the right thing to do. Besides, this was her chance to show that she belonged. She would make it work with her four: her fabulous mathematician, the daddy, herself and the stoner boy who… was… staring over her shoulder.

"Um, what are you doing?"

"What I do best. Details."

"I can't work like this." The last thing she wanted was the weakest link staring over her shoulder while she sifted through code she barely understood and… why was he sifting through his phone?

He found the picture he was looking for, and held up the phone to her while he crouched at the laptop in front of her, still staring at the code. "I told you. It helps me focus." She looked on in shock at a picture of chainmail draped over a mannequin. "I made it. It took me two months, link by link."

"This is amazing."

"Not really, when I can spend five, six, eight hours at a time doing the same thing over and over again." He moved her cursor to a line of numerical values where the hit point classes were defined. A long list of numbers, commas and semicolons jumbled together. "Every world is built this way. Brick by brick. Number by number." He started breaking apart the lines, working the single line of code into a functioning multi-line code and separating each number into a line of their own. "And… here's your brick."

He typed a single comma into a line that wasn't like the others. The only line that held a number without a comma, he added the comma in and then compiled with a shortcut keystroke she didn't even know the complier used. The command prompt blinked below with a single word: TRUE.

There are certain people you don't think you'll learn something from. Caro never imagined Lars to come to the rescue, and yet here he was, smiling humbly and offering to take her through the three subroutines he had meticulously worked out while she frantically pored over her misstep. Every line of code was meticulously laid out and commented, some with only the comment, 'this bad boy stays until the little dude on line 5 changes.' He tried to talk her into partaking, but she somehow doubted she'd be as effective and careful as he had shown himself to be.

For now, things progressed with their engineering project at a snail's pace compared to the leaps and bounds that Aidan and Wil managed in the downtown dungeon. They pooled some of the graduate programmers with the studio art majors to put together the rough skeleton of the room that they would pitch to the chamber of commerce in one week. They temporarily worked around the Death Certificate by including a remote control that a referee could use to mark anyone, monsters or players, as dead. Caro knew that the better part of her Saturday and Sunday would be spent there as they prepared for the initial run-through on Wednesday. She would have to create a world for the business men who would show up with no expectations. She was sure she could wow them. That was what she loved most about the downtown dungeon. Everyone got a story, and everyone got to walk through it.

SEVENTEEN

Caro stood at the doors to the downtown dungeon, amazed at what a few short weeks had been able to accomplish. An enterprising art student's logo put calligraphy on the glass doors, giving a "Ye Olde" feeling to the brand new equipment. Inside, walking squares tiled the floors, so that every step relayed your position back to the computerized "game master" above them. The second floor held all of the servers and controls. She would spend much of the next week designing new scenarios that customers would pay to play through. For now, though, one great scenario would have to be enough.

In less than half an hour, the chamber of commerce would be stopping by to give their final approval. The chamber thrived in the small town, populated by local business owners hell bent against liquor stores near the campus, large chains more than a block from the interstate, and generally against anything new that might take away from the old money and the established companies that became the staple of their community.

She fiddled at her clothing nervously. She felt strangely out of place in her pants suit. She never tried talking about orcs and dragons and dungeons while dressed like an adult. Still, she needed to find some way to make it appealing to someone other than students if there was any chance to make it past the people she expected to arrive at any minute.

She worked through several options, most of them getting squashed as soon as they came to the table. She vetoed anything resembling demons because of the religious backbone that lived in here in North Louisiana. Aidan vetoed everything magic, saying that accusations of black magic stifled early games and was still very much alive today, fresh in the memories of the older crowd. The rest of the group spent an hour putting up ideas and getting shot down until finally Caro settled on the idea of a tournament.

No monsters, no magic and no demons would show up. The six members of the chamber of commerce would each get to choose to go against the computer or against each other in swordplay. The robot wouldn't need to look like anything necessarily nefarious, because a fighting tournament was easily enough made to look like a historical event.

When they finally arrived, the five men and one woman in their business suits looked even more intimidating than she imagined. Aidan was the first to greet them. Wil, Aidan and Evie put so much work into it, they insisted on coming for the pitch to show each person's expertise. Aidan welcomed them with a hardy handshake and showed them into the building while the story ran through Caro's head. She did her best not to feel like a child at a science fair. This was a business, and she would show them how it could change the face of their small town for the better.

Just as the group assembled, a familiar face joined the crowd as Dr. Dietrich stepped out of a black 4x4 pickup. His gruff, stubbled persona filled her with a sense of dread. She couldn't shake the feeling that she was being graded in addition to being judged. As Aidan made the introductions, Dr. Dietrich walked up to Caro and smiled. "Relax, kid. I'm not here to throw any kind of a wrench in your plans, I assure you." He wore a fake smile that unsettled her. "I know these people. I've read your progress reports. I'm just here to put a more… permanent light on the work you're doing here."

His uninvited presence couldn't be avoided. Send him away, and she might hurt her grade, as well as hurting her chances of getting the Live Dungeon off the ground. She instead opened the door for him, resolving to watch him closely.

"We originally started with plain brick walls," Aidan walked as he talked, using great hand gestures as he spoke. You're not conducting a symphony, she groaned to herself. Get it together. As if on cue, Aidan stuck one hand on his pocket as he ran the other hand over the foam walls. "We've added sound-proofing that will eventually be covered to look like a forest scenario. By year three, we expect to have changeable panels to reflect any desired surrounding."

The older group nodded approvingly. It seemed like it was working so far, but they had yet to make it to the demonstration. She figured if she could get them to play the game, anyone could play.

They made their way along the wall to the back corner where a rack originally used for pool cues once sat. The stained wood was painted with a rusty steel texture, and batons of varying length filled the holes.

Aidan handed the greatest of the batons, a 30-ounce black rod that was over five feet long, to a stout gray-haired man in a tweed jacket. His salt-and-pepper beard turned to a frown. "What's this supposed to be?"

"We're calling this the claymore. It's slow. Look here," he pointed at a row of buttons and lights. Three buttons laid along one end of the rod, with four lights on top. "The three buttons will be different types of attacks. When the top light shows green, you'll be able to aim again. Just position your body toward your opponent and push the attack button.

The bearded man shifted toward a tall, lanky gentleman and he pushed the button. A single red light blipped quickly. "A miss?"

"That's it. A miss is registered when you're not facing a legal target, like the monster or someone who is labeled as an enemy. In this case, he doesn't have a weapon so it's like he's not there. Here you go." Aidan handed a long curved rod to the lanky man, showing him the buttons in the middle. "This is a bow. You'll be able to do the same things, but you don't have to stand in a square next to them to attack. As long as you can see them, you can attempt an attack."

"It hardly seems fair," the tall skinny man suggested. "How could the sword ever win?"

"Oh, when everything is moving, you'll see just how chaotic it becomes. Everyone's got a shot." Aidan faced the bow at the heavyset bearded man and pushed a button. A buzz sounded from the bow, and two small lights flashed twice. "A hit, and a decent one, but you can imagine the claymore might hurt a little more than two small flashing lights when it registers a solid hit."

Dr. Dietrich hovered between active participant and eager endorser. He looked over the rest of the rack of weapons, holding one of the shorter batons close to himself. "This is top notch equipment. Mr. Aidan, where did you say that you procured these?"

"The batons are from a remote control company that specializes in home entertainment systems. We've used their IR settings to register values specific to each weapon, making a choice of weapon much more tactical." Aidan walked the group over to the weapons rack and went over more of the specifics on cost as Caro questioned her impromptu guest.

"I'm sorry, professor," she held out her hands to take back the wand, "but so far our simulations only allow for a maximum of four players in a scenario at a time." His sickly sweet aftershave wafted to her as he barely contained his disappointment.

"Of course. Yes. Fascinating work, Ms. Caro. Although, I have to ask, what made you choose a remote control company over of a weapons simulator company? Surely the options available to you through combat simulation could be–"

"Well beyond the scope of this project, professor." He irked her, partly because he seemed too eager to take a leading role in her pet project, and partly because she was a little embarrassed that she hadn't considered all of the options. The game was just that – a game. The IR sensors and controllers that were currently being most widely used seemed like the most practical route.

Aidan handed the rest of the weapons out as Wil excused himself to go upstairs and load the setting. As the lights went down, huge rocks from the other back corner began to slide into place on squares that lit up red.

"Alright, take your places everyone." Caro took a deep breath and tried to take in her surroundings. The redheaded businesswoman took up a stick that detached into two small swords. She smiled picturing her assassin in this playground. The Styrofoam walls melded into throngs of cheering visitors. The oldest businessman's sword and shield baton melded into heavy armor, his gray beard hanging under his helmet. The redheaded assassin's clothing formed around her, slightly more conservative than Caro would have imagined for herself. The claymore-wielding Scot was painted with the blood of his enemies that ran off his leather armor. His choice, not Caro's. Finally the tall lanky man's archery outfit resembled Orlando Bloom a little too much. "Are you a fan, sir?"

He grinned sheepishly, then took his place behind one of the boulders. He was the first of the bunch to smile, and it felt good to get a sign of approval.

"Okay. The rules are simple. Push the attack button while you face the opponent you want to strike. Your baton will keep track of direction. When you've registered enough hits against you, I'll signal you and you'll go dark. Boys," she winked to the redhead, "go easy on the girl, will you?"

From behind his boulder, the ranger shifted into view of the oldest of the group. Counting on him to be the slowest, he took careful aim and let loose. Two lights lit up. The arrow whooshed through the air, hitting him in the leg.

The old man moved forward, shield in hand, and got close enough to strike. The waiting lights were still sounding on the bow as the sword cut into him. Five lights, a critical hit! Caro waved her wand at the archer and his square went dark. The tournament field was down to three. Somewhere above them, the heraldry marks that also appeared on the archer's tunic were taken down from the tournament standings. The blue wolf on the Scot's leather armor was at the bottom, next to the assassin's serpent. The old man's lion crest moved to the top of the board.

With the archer out of the way, there was no way to come out on top without getting closer to the others. The lion squared off against the wolf as they traded blows, his lighter sword scoring small hit after small hit as the slow claymore bounced time and time again off the shield and armor. Caro looked over to her redheaded counterpart in the corner. The one that she thought she shared so much in common with just sat there, looking bored and confused.

"Guys, this just isn't going to work."

The serpent dissipated as the playing field faded all around them. The redhead walked toward the two men, both of their black batons blinking from low health. She held her two smaller batons out in front of her. "Do you really think you'll buy this? Do you see yourselves here on the weekends, huffing and puffing to keep up with the kids?"

Caro saw her dreams crashing around her. If she couldn't sell the product as an all-ages game that the old money of this small town could get behind, would everything she accomplished die in vain? "It's more than just a game," she pleaded. "This is–"

"Silliness, really." The businesswoman held up her hand to silence Caro. The redheaded lady wasn't in her corner by herself anymore. She was standing next to the other two men, shaking her head and tsking. She pushed a button on each baton, striking the final blow to both of the men at the same time "What makes you think that either of you stood any chance, going up against a girl gamer?" Two squares went dark. The final lit square belonged to this mystery redhead.

"Miss Caro," she turned to her, "I do hope that next time you'll give the boys a better head start. I do hate to see boys cry."

"I… yes ma'am."

The other three men laughed sheepishly. Wil ran down the stairs ecstatic, "Did you see that? Two in one round! I've never seen anything like it! That was amazing! That was–"

"That was exactly what one might expect from a woman who rises to the top in a man's world." The redheaded lady smiled, "Poor boys. You are too easy to read. Perhaps next time it will be a fair fight." She turned to Caro, finally. "You can have the approval of the chamber of commerce. Be careful, though. Students have a way of spoiling the liberties that this town gives them. The first sign of trouble, or endangering the health or life of the people of this town," she warned, "we'll yank your business license and see to it that nothing like this ever comes up in this town again."

Caro thought about the living system, the user-generated

missions and the freedom she wanted to give to the people playing and designing the game. For the first time, she worried if she was doing the right thing.

"Oh, and Dietrich," the redhead added, "Good work. I see you've been truly challenging our students. See that they stay out of trouble."

Professor Dietrich gave a half-salute to her as she walked away, giving a stern glance to the students already loading up into the vehicles. "Ms. Caro," he called out as she moved to leave, "You heard the lady. Keep your nose clean. You can bet that I'll be keeping a close eye on this one. And boys? I'll be checking her code. No freebies on this one, and no conflicts of interest. Sink or swim, her side will be her side."

Caro pushed his words of caution to the back of her mind as they left from the downtown dungeon to eat chicken wings and sit down for a raucous meal of celebration and appreciation. She did well, even though she brought attention to herself and to her project far too early. She knew that she faced a difficult task ahead of her, but the team came together, and she didn't doubt that they would be up for the challenge.

EIGHTEEN

Caro walked the grounds of the most fantastic, elaborate world she had ever seen built. She tried to compare it to her campaigns, but the work that Aidan, Wil, Chad and Evie put in to make this world theirs was truly astounding. She was a bit surprised when Chad showed up, eager to help build this new machine into the universe they all knew it could become. Even before the trip to the club, he had always been quiet, but since the night club he had seemed even more distant, rarely initiating conversation and only being a cursory member of game nights.

She ran through setting after setting, first brushing her hands through the fields of Aglethorn, where Wil chose to raise his owlbears and start a tribal society. The Elven tribes lived there in peaceful harmony with the neighboring villages, but had often scrapped with adventurers who rarely treated the pristine sacred plains with the respect that they demanded.

She walked on into the mountains of Gith, where Aidan created grand scenarios dominated with winged men who ruled the skies. The Winged Ones even started up their own commerce system that interacted with the rest of the play universe while the building was closed. This AI trading community used a currency disconnected from the standard currency in the rest of the realms, and followed trends vaguely reminiscent of bitcoins.

The grandest, most sinister region was Chad's dark woods of Berth. The perils he had placed were truly frightening. She imagined the rest of his mind might be just as morbid, and looking for a way to rise to the surface. Still, the curses placed on his lands prevented his precious lizard men from straying too far into other lands. Which was good, because the Celtic buggane that Evie placed to keep her cabbit populations down were a fierce race, but still Caro would have hated to see a war inside the machine without the input of the players. All in all, the five of them created a pretty good countryside to play in, and she loved seeing the options open up before her to start creating scenarios in preparations for the first players.

She knew who the first players should be. She even extended them a special invitation.

Three days later, Caro, Evie, Aidan and Wil lined up along the sidewalk in front of the Live Dungeon as a beat up Volkswagen van rolled to a squeaky stop. It had been almost three months since she had crawled dungeons with her old friends, and she was impressed to see her favorite game master losing weight and looking cheerful as ever, even though his clothes weren't fitting him quite like they used to. He smiled big when he saw her and they embraced tightly. Jude and Jeremy stepped off after, in full soccer regalia. She figured they had been streaming Premier league soccer the whole way. The twins walked up to the front doors, giving Caro each a sideways hug while trying to take everything in.

"This is going on Facebook." Jude snapped a picture as Jeremy swatted his hand.

"Seriously, man. Can't you ever just be in the moment?" Jeremy walked over to the weapons rack, eyeing the display next to it. "Is this it?"

"Yep." Caro turned on the display, bringing up drop down menus for each of the options they created. "So far, we've only got options for each of the four base weapons, dual wielding, ranged weapon, two handed sword, and sword and shield. The apps are all written using open source technology, so we hope to have more options for full characters soon." She walked them through the choices and set them up with their weapons of choice.

"So where do you want to go?"

The dark woods of Berth swarmed with trolls hiding behind every boulder, bush and massive gnarled oak. Every step risked raising the beasts from their slumber. Jeb's Barbarian pushed through the brambles and around trees as they searched for the lost temple of Uruhil. Jeremy's Ranger kept his distance, keeping an eye on the rear of the party with his bow leveled far ahead of the barbarian's lead position. Jude's Scout walked alongside the main trail, skipping silently through the rough forest terrain with ease, his swords drawn in front of him.

Through the wind rustling the leaves of the lush forest, the barbarian heard the bounding footsteps of the great troll-king Fritzl as he frantically searched the forest for intruders. He sniffed the air as he ran forward, unaware that they stood just twenty feet from the head of the party of heroes. The barbarian signaled to the other two to stay close as he hid behind a rock. The troll king stopped dead when the faint smell of human flesh wafted up into his great green nostrils.

His massive arm swept from behind him as he roared his battle cry, fanning his elite guard out in front of him. From far behind the advancing troops, the trouble they would have to go through to collect his head had just increased exponentially.

The three elite troll guards crept past the barbarian unaware, searching through the thick woods for signs of something amiss. The ranger leveled his bow on the smallest one, hoping for a quiet take down. The arrow grazed the troll guard's shoulder and he howled in rage. Two of the three guards fell on the barbarian, while the third tromped further into the woods looking for the bow that shot the arrow.

As the third guard cleared the scout's position, Jude's twin blades crept up behind one of the two trolls facing the barbarian. He struck swiftly, severing first an arm, and then the head of the unsuspecting guard. One on one, the barbarian made short work of the other guard pounding past his defenses with strong, slow and arcing strokes.

The third guard reached the scout's position just as the bow was readied again. They attacked at the same time, the arrow passing the blade and both scoring devastating hits. The ranger's bow was faster, though, and made quick work of the troll before he could come around again for another swing.

The three faced off against the troll king alone, lining up behind the barbarian's great sword. As the king moved forward, the barbarian came straight in and the scout moved behind him to flank. The ranger *stepped to the side to get a clearer line of sight, hiding behind the boulder for extra cover. The troll king swung his heavy club at the barbarian, who dodged deftly and countered with his great sword. The scout worked swiftly from behind, taking advantages of the cracks in the monstrosity's thick hide. Every time the ranger saw an opening, he let another arrow fly, always high, and always sure to stay clear of his shorter allies in the fight even though many of his higher shots went wide of the troll.*

After several rounds of epic battle, the troll and barbarian were nearing death. Their regular swings came less frequently, and they dodged less often. The barbarian summoned what strength that remained to drive the sword through the trolls head from under, but it was too slow. The troll's massive club bore down on him, driving him into the mud below. The scout made quick work of the troll as he was still turned and unable to match speed with the scout's swift blades. The ranger got a few shots in, too, before the lights went up on the end of the mission.

"Not bad," Jeb smiled, already breathing a little heavy. Twenty minutes in the room turned out to be enough for a quick encounter, and by stringing those encounters together, Caro planned to be able to take people through epic, arcing storylines. Jeb returned his large baton to the weapons rack. "So how big of a world are we talking about?"

She went through the database with him, going over the areas that the other four created. They talked through possibilities, but Jeb just shook his head. "I can't get over it. This is fantastic, but this isn't the world I was imagining when you told me you were building something expansive."

"Well," Caro backpedaled a little. "I mean, it's not big yet, but it will be. Anyone can add to the world. We've set up a content management solution that allows buildings, terrain, people and monsters to be added into the system. All content is approved by an administrator, but as long as there are people who have a story to tell, they can use our dungeon."

Jeb was intrigued. "I'll help you build your world, Caro. Just promise me you'll remember me when you're big and famous." He laughed to himself as his eyes trailed off. "Absolutely amazing."

Jude and Jeremy stayed the night, making more character options and customizing the weapons for each new face. Jeb stayed for another four days to see more of the world, and add in some of his more elaborate villains and allies. On the third day, Evie came by in a long black dress and heavy coat looking for Caro.

"You've been working too hard. I figure it's time to take you out of here." Caro was approving more of the changes Jeb made. They were all remarkable, even if some of the puzzles seemed a little obscure. She nodded in that tired way that told volumes about how she barely possessed the energy to do much more. "This can wait. What happens if they go on without you for a few hours?"

Jeb looked up from his touch screen at the scene before him. "Who's this?"

"Oh, this is Evie. My… roommate." Somehow the word didn't feel like enough. Evie put her hands on her hips in playful indignation. "I mean, she's my – well–"

"No surprise there," Jeb smirked. "I always figured if the right one came along..."

Caro was indignant. Jeb always pretended to know more than he really did in that cocky self-satisfied way. She pointed a finger at him, annoyed at the accusation, "No way. You couldn't have known. I never knew!"

"Relax. I just meant, hell, anyone. Boys didn't ignite that spark in you. Certainly not your ex." Evie squeezed Caro's hand and gave her a comforting look. "In four years of being around you, I've never seen anyone who could leave you stuttering. I'm just happy for you, that's all."

"Well, thank you."

"Still, I called it." Jeb could be infuriating.

NINETEEN

The pre-opening day was supposed to be a chance to try out the scenarios that were submitted, and to give people a chance to tell Caro and Aidan what they thought of the business. More and more, Aidan became the go-to for all things business. His head for keeping things palatable for the masses became a huge advantage, as well as his advanced experience at surviving the studying bonanza that led up to finals week. In the end, half of the decisions ended up being controlled by him, and the rest by the board of business students that had worked up the proposal. At least, that was until Caro's mother showed up.

Until then, her mother had only taken a passive interest in the project, checking in regularly only to see a bottom line. Occasionally they spent Sunday Skype conversations catching up on everyday life and the random question about how things were progressing. Once the project topped ten thousand dollars, though, she put her foot down, insisting on an active voice in the decisions that she felt would spiral expenses over Caro's budget. A week before this pre-opening day, she wanted to know what would happen when the first group of customers were brought in.

She suggested bringing in a trial group of people under factors that could be controlled, but insisted that they be the kind of random people that might normally sign up for an event like it. She hoped, she told them, that they might somehow have a sample opening night that they could have more control over rather than the first night where they open the doors to the public. Caro agreed.

They put up flyers around the middle school, on the college campus and through church youth groups around town to see what kind of a crowd they might draw. In the end, they settled on four groups to run sessions for a total of two hours. They assumed it would give them plenty of time to set up the room in between sessions. The walkway ended up turning into a staging area where options could be chosen while the previous game was still running, and a viewing area where they could see how the other groups performed.

Despite all the indications that they were being supervised closely, it was hard to keep the children from getting out of hand. One of the batons got broken in the second session, and one of the robots needed to be repaired for structural damage when an especially enthusiastic little boy thought that swinging the claymore was a much better way of determining if there was a hit. An especially rowdy crowd from the college came in drunk and stumbled their way through the session, knocking over a boulder and ending the day early. All in all, four thousand dollars in equipment was damaged, while they expected to only get around eight hundred dollars in revenue.

After they sent everyone home, Aidan banged away at the frame of one of the robots while Evie patched a boulder with stucco. "This is never going to work," Aidan mumbled through gritted teeth. He used a metal file to pry a section of the robot's frame back in place. Evie smiled her best optimistic smile, but just sucked her teeth in agreement.

"We can do this," Caro pushed them. "I mean, this is what happens when people who aren't gamers play a new game, right? How much do you think arcades spend every month in repairs?"

"Definitely less than they make," Aidan offered. "Maybe we could make them sturdier?" They found a way to pad everything, even the rods. IR sensors were covered in cheap plastic to protect them, but the rest of the batons were covered in foam. Monsters were coated in thicker plastics to prevent damage to the metal frames, and the tiles, while still intact, were reinforced with Plexiglas covers just in case. Evie was even able to make up a big rules board to make it easier to explain what was and wasn't acceptable, and to keep the troublemakers in line with threats of being forced to leave or being eaten by trolls.

Two days later, they were back in business and running more smoothly. Caro worked out a deal with a nearby smoothie shop to exchange coupons once business was in full swing, and she already started to consider buying the aging building next door in hopes of opening up a second room one day. That weekend, Jeb, Jeremy and Jude even came back up to run another few sessions and Caro's mom showed up in person to take a look at the layout.

"We're really doing it," she told Aidan one day as she looked over the numbers. "This place could actually make money one day." She sat against the wall, exhausted from a full night of work and getting anxious about finals. "There's just one thing I can't figure out, though. Where is all of this content coming from?"

"Oh, I opened it up to online submissions."

"That sounds like a terrible idea." Something about online submissions reminded her of the torrential flooding of fanfiction that found its way into every new fad. "Have you played through them? Are they terrible? How do we know they're any good?"

Aidan shrugged. "Got a minute? Let's go through a couple! Maybe we can start assigning challenge ratings."

It sounded good. Caro was so exhausted with putting together scenarios, studying for finals and surviving on little sleep that she strained to remember the last time she escaped into her make-believe worlds. "Sure. Let's do it. I want to get Evie in on this, though. Just wouldn't feel right without her." She texted Evie, then shuffled through player options as she shook the cobwebs from her brain. The list was growing like crazy, and she ended up having to narrow her choices with a search function before she could decide on a rogue. Evie came in and hugged her, then found her own knight as Aidan loaded up a random scenario.

The building lights dimmed as a roiling pit of lava started to edge toward them.

Aidan's sorcerer joined them as the lava circle kept getting smaller and smaller. Glowing blue runes appeared on each of the monster faces, with a single pentagram in the middle of the room. The computer voice boomed from the loudspeakers. "Three minutes to volcanic eruption. Remove the curse and live."

The walls darkened, and traces of cooled volcanic rock edged the outside of the room, but still too far away to reach from where they were herded. Evie held her sword and shield close, looking for some sort of way out, or some rhyme or reason to the runes that floated on the heads around them. "I don't like this one. Let's get out of here." She stepped toward the far wall, expecting to see the life drain from the black rod and show her character as dying. Instead, an electric arc burst up from the floor and sent her diving away and crying out in pain. She limped away, heading toward the control room.

Caro dropped her weapon too as she moved toward the board to reset the room, but Aidan held fast. "I can get it."

"Don't be ridiculous. We don't even know what the hell is going on here." Caro's voice raised an octave as the room seemed darkened and the voice boomed a warning about removing curses again. "Aidan, just let it go."

Aidan turned to the first rune, a green rune resembling alpha and shot a magic bolt at it. Part of the Lava slowed, leaving an oblong section closing in on him. He hit the second rune, a red pi symbol, and it just turned a bright orange. When he hit the third symbol, a silver phi symbol, the lava started to close in again. It inched to where he was standing, and current jumped through his feet as his wracked body writhed in pain. He moved to the center of the room and put his hands on the pentagram, studying it carefully.

He must have known he had seconds left before the pain would come again. Why the hell didn't he just get out of there? Caro's frustration bubbled over as she pleaded for him to stop again.

Aidan looked over the shimmering pentagram again, studying the changing patterns. He hit the alpha again, and then he pointed his wand at the pi symbol again, shooting once, twice... over and over again. The rune shifted colors from red to orange, yellow to green and all the way through to a deep violet before the lava stopped completely. Alpha, then all the colors of the rainbow, but it's not over until...

Aidan drew a deep breath. He pointed his wand toward the black omega symbol and shot one final time. The lights went up, the lava moved back to the outer edge and the seal opened up. "Thank you for playing." The computer voice boomed as the three looked at each other warily. "New challenge unlocked."

The three raced upstairs to look at the database. "Who did that?" Caro was furious, and doing her best to calm Evie's spasming legs.

Aidan sifted through the records. "I've never heard of him. Lord Defiler. Did you approve him?"

"Absolutely not. I haven't managed users in... hell, I don't know how long," she pushed back her tears. "I'm so sorry, Evie. We can fix this."

Evie shrank back. "I don't get it. How could they do this? How could they make the game dangerous? I thought it was supposed to be safe."

Aidan looked through the code for the weapons. "This is some crazy stuff. This variable... it looks like they rerouted power through the floor sensors to cause a short, shocking the person standing on it. It's this damn tile. It normally uses this pathway with smaller voltages to determine position. We can't disable it and still run the dungeon program. He shouldn't have been able to do it, but it looks like he found a back door." Aidan went back into the main database and started running some more basic queries. "I'm deleting everything from this guy. I'm not taking any chances. Did I approve him? I mean, maybe. It's possible. So much has come through lately–"

"I don't care. As long as he's the only one. What are the odds he's got more stuff in the system?" Caro joined Aidan at the computer looking through the files.

"I was thinking the same thing. I've found everything submitted from that IP address just in case, and I'm taking it all out of the system." He stopped typing, looking at the ground between them. "There's something else..."

"That address, that's here?"

"It's local, yes. You're recognizing one of the internal IP addresses from inside the college's network. Whoever he is, he submitted this from the campus." Aidan shut down the computer and walked over to help Evie up. "We've disabled all new submissions that aren't ours and gotten rid of everything on his workspace. I think we're okay for now."

"I wouldn't be so sure," Caro suggested. "It seems to me like he wanted to make a statement. He wanted to see if he was smarter than us. Odds are pretty good that the new challenge that we unlocked will surface in the next few days. Let's keep an eye on it, and keep Wil upstairs to make sure this doesn't happen again, and even if it does, he can shut it down on a moment's notice."

Evie got up and walked toward the door. "You guys are nuts. Shut it down before someone else gets hurt. You heard the Chamber. They're going to string you up if they find out this happened."

Caro tried to calm her down, but it was no use. There was no comforting her, even though what looked like every trace of the Lord Defiler was wiped from the system. Just talking to her was getting more difficult as Evie grew more distant while nursing her legs. That night was the quietest night in the dorm room in a long time, and Caro just wished Evie would talk to her.

TWENTY

Caro straightened Patrick's tie while Juneau went through her presentation notes. Lars still hadn't arrived, and Caro was on the edge of fury expecting the worst. She talked to him the day before, and he knew that the only thing he was required to do was bring a button-down shirt and tie, and sit in the back and look interested while the rest of the group presented the work. He pulled through for her on debugging the code, but other than that hadn't provided much help. When they finally decided on splitting the presentation up, they gave him introductions. Surely, he couldn't mess that up. They were five minutes away from presentation, though, and he still hadn't showed.

Most of the projects in the classroom seemed to be put together fairly well. The limitations of the robots and imaginations of the students reflected on each of them. A parking assist was created. It wasn't even the good kind that helped you parallel park without crashing. It just scanned an area to see if there were still parking spots available. The limitations were glaring. Another group came up with a way to find out how fast you were going by using an accelerometer. The integration of using a single sensor must have taken… minutes. Looking around the room, Caro liked her odds. She needed to do well on this to make it out of the class. She didn't like that her grade would be the same as Lars' grade, but she swallowed her sense of fairness and seethed while watching the door for any sign of him.

The presentation that preceded them barely finished when a clean cut Lars walked through the door. His sharp navy blue suit sat crisp against his strides, hair trimmed neatly and cheeks oily from a fresh shave. He looked every bit the part of a boyish prince. She couldn't deny that he cleaned up nice, despite her aggravation with his unreliability bubbling up inside. He handed a stapled stack of papers to the professor and made his way to the group as they put everything in place in the front of the class.

"What the hell were you doing?" Caro scolded.

"No one read the presentation requirements, so I took the liberty." He motioned to the professor who sat looking through the paperwork. "That's the printout of our code you're looking at. Without it, he'd probably just assumed we copied and pasted something to make our sensors work." He stood hands in pockets and eyebrows raised, "Well? If you're not going to apologize, I'll take a simple 'thank you'."

Caro turned to Juneau. "How did we miss this? That's... that's impossible."

Juneau just shrugged and grabbed Lars by the arm. "Thank you. Good job."

"Okay, Team Eight. Let's hear it." It was the last team of the day, and Professor Dietrich's patience was waning. "We're all ready to go home, I'm sure."

After Lars introduced the team, Caro presented a section on the problem itself, along with similar solutions which compared the Death Certificate program to interfacing software that dealt with multiple proprietary systems, breaking down information to automate large sections of batch chemical plants and assembly factories. When they got to the solution, Juneau walked the class through the basic steps of the code, and then Patrick presented the issues that they came across along the way, including the coding errors that took up so much of their time trying to fix. When the classroom lights came up, Professor Dietrich was standing in the middle of the classroom, an inquisitive hand raised.

A pit of worry started to form in Caro's stomach. "Um, yes, Professor Dietrich?"

"This is some good work here." He held up the code that was used on the robot. "Hell, I haven't seen code like this in three years. Who worked on the code?"

"We all did." Lars stood proud, puffed chest.

Damnit, Lars. Why can't you keep your mouth shut?

"I see, Mr. Lars. Well, that's good to hear. Tell me, which part did you work on?"

"I helped to proofread the code, so I got a good look at all of it."

Why was he making it worse?

"Ah, good. I see here that your team used a FOR loop to check for the state of the, er, hit points as you called them. Can you tell me why you would use that instead of a WHILE loop?"

Lars didn't miss a beat. "We used the FOR loop instead of the WHILE loop to have better control in how often we were checked the status of the hit points. In the end, the choice was largely one of preference, and the hit points were still being checked at 16 Hertz, which was well within latency requirements due to the reaction times of user inputs."

Son of a bitch, he's got it. Caro smiled broadly at the surprising turn of events. Apparently he did more than just print it off, and the time that he spent staring at the computer screen wasn't truly wasted. He just might have saved her grade. She felt the rising waters recede a little.

"And, Miss Caro. I see that this project you're working on now will be used on your dungeon downtown. Have you given any thought to backdoor protocols, and how to prevent hacking to your system?"

It hardly seemed fair. The rest of the groups answered one question at the most, and it invariably seemed to deal with some minor nuance that struck him as curious. Not only did he just ask a second question, but both seemed to be aimed directly at struggling students, and technical questions that they might not have known an answer to. On top of that, the recent hacking of the rods was still fresh in her mind. He couldn't have known about the Lord Defiler program, could he? Her eyes narrowed. She studied him carefully, looking for some sinister pleasure that he might be taking from this.

His eyebrows raised, and he flipped through the pages of code as his voice took on a darker tone. "Miss Caro. I need an answer to my question."

"No, Professor. Nothing has been put in place to prevent such an attack." She searched for a grin, or anything that might betray him. She couldn't imagine this as the Lord Defiler, though. It didn't make any sense. What did he have against any of his students, and why would he want to hurt them?

"Thank you. I'll see you all next week when you turn in any borrowed equipment." Chairs shuffled, backpacks went onto the tables as everyone started packing to leave. It was ten minutes before the class would normally end, but the students didn't put up any fight to stay.

As the rest of the class shuffled out, Caro walked up to her professor sitting at his desk, going through the presentation grading rubrics. She knew she needed to phrase herself carefully, because she didn't want to accuse him before he issued a final grade for the semester. "Do you know something about the Live Dungeon that you're not telling me?"

"Miss Caro, I follow all of my students' work related to engineering. I can assure you, I have no idea specifically what you might be referring to. Is there something going on there?"

She decided to go a different route. "What do you know about the Live Dungeon?"

"It's impressive work. It's good that you've brought something into this town that so many of the students are drawn to. It's quite an accomplishment. I just wonder what will happen to your dungeon when you graduate."

Caro hadn't given it much thought. Here in her first year, graduation seemed a lifetime away. "It will always be there. I could even see passing it on to another generation of students to take care of it. It could very well be my legacy to this fine institution." She smiled at the thought of passing her creation on. Everyone was so passionate about putting it together, making it better and making it a little bit theirs, she figured it would be easy enough to find people to take over after she left.

"That's absurd. A business run by a revolving door of managers? One bad manager can make or break a company. Have you seen some of the students that walk through this door? I assure you, you wouldn't allow this business model to exist if you only–"

"I've seen them." That aftershave hung in her nostrils, emboldening her. "I've seen what they can do when they find something they love, and that's the kind of managers that will always keep the company going." Caro had bit her tongue so long, she thought it wiser to let loose and lose a few points on her grade than keep it in and swallow blood. "Just this semester, I've seen what it could do for Lars. Did you ever think he would make it, given where he stood at midterms?"

"He didn't make it."

"I'm sorry?"

"He didn't make it. Look, I'm not supposed to tell you this, but you should know that your little team member isn't going to pass the class." He shifted in his chair uncomfortably. "I'm not sure why he bothered to show up today at all."

"Because he had hope," Caro started to cry. If he didn't make it, what chance did she have?

"He had no hope. I told him two weeks ago that no matter what he made on this project, he was out. That's why he stopped coming to class. I assumed it was the last I'd seen him. This happens to half of the students I teach every semester."

Lars stuck it out for them, but she couldn't imagine why. They didn't treat him in any way he deserved. She didn't want to ask, but the words came out of her mouth anyway, "What about me? Did I pass?"

"We'll see." Professor Dietrich shrugged noncommittally. She slunk off, defeated. If she couldn't hack it at the beginning, she doubted there was any place for her in the rest of the program.

TWENTY-ONE

By day, Professor Dietrich's words haunted her every thought. When she slept, she dreamt of the Lord Defiler. She tried to escape into work, but less and less people were coming every day. Many of the random scenarios that were submitted seemed to be impossible battles and puzzles that she couldn't seem to shake. She called up Jeb to take a look at some of the puzzles, thinking that possibly they were written for a more serious gamer. He took a trip up the next weekend to run through the puzzle scenarios.

Going in, he insisted that the puzzles would likely be small things that she had missed. After going through four of them in the regularly allotted twenty minutes, he walked out of the simulator feeling mildly triumphant.

"Sure, they're puzzles, but it's not like they're impossible to solve."

Caro was devastated. "What can we do? The kids coming in here, they don't see these puzzles as challenges. They walk into a scenario with nothing to kill, they get frustrated after a few minutes and then they walk out demanding to get their money back." She stared at the database of scenarios which hadn't grown since Wil removed the internet submissions. "I can't make them want to think. I can only give them what they want." She sighed. "I don't know. Maybe we should just delete them."

"Why the hell would you do that?" Jeb started to raise his voice. "Maybe the small minds of this small town could use a little sharpening now and then. Maybe they could afford to be a little more challenged."

"That hardly seems fair." She remembered seeing him get defensive about the difficult puzzles before. There were gaming sessions where he would present them with a challenge, often giving them little or no clues that might help them strategize or solve puzzles. He would sit behind his game master screen and fold his arms, taking joy in their squirming and frustration.

"You've got everything you need," he would often say, only to give up an hour later when everyone else got up from the table to leave. There were gamers out there like Jeb: people who would never use walkthroughs, people who would sit for days in front of a single challenge in computer games or puzzle books just to get the satisfaction of having figured something out on their own. Caro had no idea how to deal with those types of people. Her father was a gamer, but his tall stack of Nintendo Power magazines and crossword dictionaries led her to believe that most challenges that her father faced was with all the resources of the great minds who came before him. She tried to remember the last video game she finished without a walkthrough, but none came to mind.

"I don't get it," she conceded. "Obviously whoever made these challenges wanted to challenge a different group of people from the typical customers we get here. I'll go through them the best that I can, and the ones that seem impossible will have to be archived. Let me know next time you come through. If you're feeling squirrely, you're welcome to go through more of them."

"Let them come. Let them fail." Jeb was nonplussed. Caro didn't like the sound of that at all. She saw more refunds in her future. "The real gamers will respect you for it, and you'll have a real dungeon that's worth driving one, two or more hours just to get in."

She shook her head. He seemed to really like watching them fail. There was a glee in his eyes about it, a superiority. It wouldn't surprise her. Jeb would take any opportunity to feel superior to people. For him, living in a bigger city seemed enough. Casual gamers dying in the dungeon was like a bonus.

"I'll tell you what," she offered. "Take your time tomorrow. Go through as many as you want. You can come in for free if you'll just rate them for me and let me know what our small brains aren't ready for." For now, she would have to give him the satisfaction to help her narrow down the hundreds of scenarios that were approved into the system. Why on earth did Aidan approve so many? She would have to talk to him about that.

She left Jeb at the dungeon to go find Aidan. She had been by his house once or twice, a small rent house on the outskirts of town. The small home sat on an overgrown piece of property with weeds crawling up the sides of a small stone porch. She knocked on the door, but no one answered. Aidan's car was in the driveway, so she pushed on the door which opened easily. She called out when she came in, and that's when she heard the shower going. She called out a little louder and Aidan announced that he would be out in a minute. She walked through the living room to the kitchen area.

From there, three doors to the nearby bedrooms ended the hallway to the east side of the house. Two of them were closed, but a single door was cracked and through it she could see a large silicone dragon's head hanging on the wall. Her curiosity got the best of her and she opened the door more. Next to the dragon's head was a katana with an ivory handle, complete with red eyes and wings on the hilt. The bedspread that was crumpled at the foot of the bed was a fire breathing black dragon, which made her laugh. The gamers that she knew would have known better. Black dragons breathe acid. The more she walked around the small room, the more she saw dragon everything.

She came to a small diorama of a knight slaying a dragon with a small bowl for jewelry in it. The strangest thing about the diorama wasn't that the jewelry bowl wasn't empty, but that there was a small silver ring in the middle of it. Evie's mother's small silver ring sat there, surrounded by a few pennies and a pog. Bile rose up in her throat, and she felt a rage that bordered somewhere between livid and nauseous.

Aidan stepped out of the shower in a lush red robe with flowers on it. "What are you doing in here," Aidan looked at her out of the corner of his eye.

She held up the ring, anger bubbling over. "What is this doing here? Whose room is this? How long have you known this was here?" Her knees were starting to feel weak. She felt herself sitting down, her body losing control.

Aidan caught her by her arms, setting her into a bean bag chair at the end of the bed. He looked at the ring as recognition set in. "This is it... That's impossible. We were all there. We searched the floors of that disgusting bar for hours." He tried to remain calm, but his body began to shake. "Oh, he's going to pay for this. But not today, not now."

"Whose room is this?" She started to tear up, not wanting to know the truth, but not wanted to be lied to anymore.

Aidan hesitated, "Promise you won't say a word just yet."

"What? No. There are only three people that live here, and you didn't have a clue that this was in here? That leaves Wil and Chad–" That son of a bitch.

She looked over to Aidan, who still held his hands out to her trying to calm her. She was nearly hyperventilating, and the realization of his last words stuck in her head. "Why the hell wouldn't I say anything to him right now? What difference does a few days make? Why would I ever try to spare his feelings?"

"You don't get it. He can't know that you found this. Not yet. Not until I know for sure." It didn't make any sense. The ring was in his room. If he hadn't stolen it, how would it have gotten here, and when it did get here, why wouldn't he have come to her as soon as he found it?

"What the hell are you talking about?"

"I think I know who's been putting the dangerous code into our program. I can't prove it's him yet, but I need him to keep acting normally until I find out more about his programs."

"That doesn't make any sense, Aidan. How does his programming have anything to do with the programs in the game? Even if it was him, he wouldn't have access to the system to add anything new." She tried to put the Lord Defiler face on Chad. "It doesn't fit, anyway. How the hell would he be able to program like that? Wil said so himself. The kind of programmer knowledge it would take to make something so deadly is years beyond what he's ever seen, and Chad's an engineering student. He's not even in computer science."

"Just trust me, and let's get out of here before he gets home." She threw the ring back into the jewelry dish. "I'll explain everything later. He should be home any minute."

They walked out of the room, and she sat in the kitchen seething while she pored over the night's events. He must have slipped the ring off her finger while she was being carried by the crowd at the bar. That meant that he put his hands on her. Her body convulsed. He had touched her. He stole something from her and Evie that meant more to them than he would ever mean to her. She would tell him soon, but she didn't like the idea of waiting. She got up from her barstool when Chad's car pulled up the driveway. Aidan walked over to the door and paused before opening it, "Not a word. I need a few more days to go through his computer to find more evidence. While he still thinks we don't know what's going on, I can still get in when he leaves it unlocked. If he has any idea that we're onto the antics he's been pulling, he'll be more on guard."

"What the hell are we supposed to do about the Live Dungeon

in the mean time? We've got to do something before we lose all of our customers, or even worse, before someone else gets hurt!" She was pleading. Catching him with enough evidence to put him away would be nice, but she would much rather put a stop to his destruction of her dream before there was nothing worth saving.

"We'll go in together," Aidan suggested. "I can get past any riddle he's got. Your character in the system can handle any beast he can put us up against. We'll find the new challenge and get rid of it before anyone else can activate it, if it makes you feel better."

"And when he finds out we're off to defeat his precious challenge?"

"If he's the psycho I think he is, he'll welcome it. He doesn't think we can make it through anyway. I just need you to let him know we're on our way in. If he's got any way to activate it, we'll make sure that it happens on our shift." Aidan unlocked the door as Chad's car door closed. "We go in tomorrow night for the challenge to get it before the weekend starts. He'll be working on his computer up through Friday for school, so just be patient with me for two more days while I dig for more evidence, okay?"

"Fine," she muttered through gritted teeth. "After that, I'm stringing his balls up the flagpole."

TWENTY-TWO

Aidan flipped the keys casually in his hand as he walked with Caro out the front door of the small cottage home. Chad walked up the drive, looking pleasantly surprised to see the two of them together. "Hey Caro. How'd you managed to break away from studying this close to finals?"

"Oh, I found something more important that needed to be taken care of." Caro seethed under her calm composure, looking to Aidan for backup.

"Yeah, we found a glitch in the dungeon. We're just going to run through a few sessions, make sure we can fix it. No big deal."

"I can help. I've got some time."

Aidan put his hands in his pockets, "Didn't…. you say that you were going to be working on our design project all night? I just assumed you'd be in front of the computer until dawn."

Chad looked back and forth between the two of them, "Nah. I mean, I've got a long way to go before I'm finished with the design project tonight, sure, but who could pass up the chance to spend some time with my two best friends?" He gave the best smile he could manage, but it quickly dropped when neither of the other two returned the enthusiasm. "Okay. I get it. You two need some time alone. Is that it? Is something going on?"

Aidan and Caro answered differently at the same time. "No."

"Yes," Caro nodded, staring knowingly at Aidan. "Chad, I'm sorry, but Aidan and I need some time... alone."

Chad let out a disappointed harrumph, and then threw his hands into the air. "Whatever. No one ever invites me anyway. If you need me, I'll be in my room, minding my own damn business." He was sulking again, and it seemed to buy them all the time they needed. Aidan drove them downtown while Caro tried to sort it out in her head.

"I just don't get it. Chad is weird, but he's not psycho serial killer weird, right? I mean, he's not like those killers in the movies that set the traps that make people kill themselves. He's not that crazy, right?"

Aidan shook his head. "Beats me. I've known the guy for years, but I don't think I've ever really got to know this dark side he shows when he starts to crawl up into his own thoughts." They pulled into the downtown area as Aidan started to lay out a plan for the session. "If I'm going in with you, we're doing it my way. I know you don't like power gamers, but I'm not taking any chances in case that Lord Defiler trap gets sprung while we're in there." He reached over and held her hand, "This might be the only way to fix what we released in the last game, and I doubt we'll have any way out once the session starts."

"I agree, but what the hell do I know about power gaming?" It was what annoyed her most about the people who escaped into the fantasy world. Power gamers made the most of every rule, loophole, and gaming statistic to create the greatest game breaking character that was possible. Often times, when one power gamer played in a group of people, the game would devolve into a one man show.

They pulled into the parking lot and made their way to the front door. Most of the security lights lit up, even though their doorway was dark from a burned light bulb on the light at their corner. Caro pushed conspiracy theories to the back of her mind and made a mental note to call the city in the morning. She turned lights on as Aidan went to the weapons rack to pick out characters. Aidan chose a psychic warrior that Caro never let him play in their regular gaming sessions. "Is the psychic warrior too broken for you now?"

"Hell no. What do you have for me?"

Caro examined her assassin armor as the cave's magical sconces lit the way for them. The leather brocading was intricately woven. It was the finest that gold could buy. Twin enchanted bone daggers hung from her waist, their dark power emanating through her, making her feel drunk with magic. "Not bad. Not bad at all."

Aidan motioned for Caro to go first down the spooky tunnel. The moss on the walls thickened the deeper they went in, and she felt an eerie sense of déjà vu. This place seemed so familiar to her. Aidan's psychic warrior spurred her further, encouraging her. "Whatever you can't sense, disarm or dodge, I can absorb. Let's get to the end of this tunnel, that way we can put this to rest, finally." They made it all the way to the far end, and a great boulder sat at the far end where a door used to be.

"I guess this one was a dud?"

Aidan shook his head, swaying his deep purple robes as he searched the walls. "Impossible. Most of the stuff that was submitted was simple stuff, with file sizes around 38k. This file was huge. There's no way this was just an empty hallway."

"Why? How big a file are we talking about?"

Aidan's voice dropped low. "28 megs. Whatever this program isn't showing us, we've got to break through. This must be where the second challenge is hidden."

Caro activated her skills on her twin daggers to look around at the walls around them. At one far end, a monster backed up into the wall, leaving the face showing a faint red symbol. She saw the pi symbol from the Lord Defiler's last mission. "I think I've got something."

Aidan walked over to her, and started trying to engage the symbol magically. After the fourth try, he gave up and Caro stepped in front of the magical rune. She held her enchanted lock picks up to the screen, and the lights went out, leaving only the lit squares beneath them to light their way.

"Welcome, adventurers. I had so hoped you might be able to join me. Please. Do come in." The booming voice finished as the floor squares lit up, showing a new area. The new magical sconces changed. They showed the calligraphy mark of the double d. It was Dark Dugan's lair.

"No. That's not possible. I've been here before." Caro tried to remember back to her last session with her old group of friends. "This is Dark Dugan, the Lich Queen. But, how did it get here, unless Jeb has been submitting sessions into the computer. He would never hurt me. I don't get it."

"Is this your friend's work?" Aidan walked carefully across each square, stepping tentatively and prepared to jump toward a wall in case any trap was sprung. Whatever damage that might be done to his character's hit points in the database, if he could avoid the very real side effects of the Lord Defiler's tech-heavy traps, he would be prepared to move quickly. "Some friend."

Caro walked toward a far wall where a magical stone was pulsating with Morrigan the Bard's last tale. This tale was the same haunting bard song that was playing right before she left from home, right before she ruined Jeb's grand campaign, and right after she told him that she would be leaving them all behind. It seemed like a ridiculous motive, but she had been wrong about people before. She had been wrong about Chad in her scarred, recent memories of him.

"Dugan! Get out here, you old shriveled witch! I want to see you!" Caro seethed. Jeb wanted to posture, to monologue, and engage the players in a story. If that's what it took to figure out what he was up to, she'd sit through it, and drive a dagger through his heart right as soon as she was done with the Lich bitch.

"Ah, I have company after all." The dark laughter emanating from the walls could have come from anywhere. The monster pillars surrounded them, but none differentiated obstacle from foe. "Please, stay where you are. You don't want to make a false move once my security network is enabled."

The floors lit up to a deep and fiery red, resembling the magma from the last challenge. The only white tiles were those that the players and the monsters were standing on. Now that the monsters were easy enough to find, Caro could see four figures spread out in the small room around Aidan and her. Three of them showed a devil's face, and only one had the face of the evil lich that she had put to rest months before. Now, it was back and she was sure that she wouldn't be able to get out of it quickly. In the middle of the room, a green seal emanated around a five-foot square.

"What are you trying to pull, Dugan?" Caro addressed the monster directly.

"I'm not pulling anything. I'm saving you, actually. I'm saving you from my beasties, who would do anything to tear into your precious flesh." The tiles blinked on and off, along with a single tile adjacent to them. As the tiles shifted, everyone in the room moved to a new position to avoid the electrified tiles below them. Aidan readied a psychic blast, aiming at the Lich.

"No!" Caro was too late. Aidan's blast rebounded off the witch, shorting out the board underneath him and giving him a quick jolt. He let out a cry of pain and Caro tried to calm him. "I tried that. Jeb's not giving us the easy way out. We'll have to hear out his story, and then the battle will go the way he wants it to." She hated being railroaded. Even worse, she hated it when her railroading came at the cost of someone else's pain.

The lich let out a laugh as the program ran its course. "See, now here I am trying to be a good little lich, and you've gone and upset the babies. The seal that protects you protects them as well, you know. Any attempt to hurt them before you've heard me out will only make things worse for you. Now," she paused for effect, "do be a dear and listen up.

"I've gone to great lengths to bring you here, assassin. The last time we met, you called off our little meeting all too soon. I think we can still come to an agreement, though, if you'll hear me out."

"Just tell us how to get out of here."

"Well, there are two ways out, Assassin." The floor tiles blinked beneath them revealing one option to move, and it brought Aidan within striking distance of the great devil in front of him. As they moved, the devil gave into the temptation and lashed out at Aidan, giving a jolt of electricity to himself and Aidan at the same time. "Oh, my. It looks like you're getting a good feel for the first option. Leave my offer on the table, and we all suffer the same fate. This dungeon won't last forever. If you think you can outlast the Lich Queen, I will bring this building down on your head."

"And the second option?" She was just fifteen feet away from the queen, but the blinking lights sent her next steps away, and she couldn't reach for a strike, or figure out what to do next.

"The second option, is that you join me. Throw your weapons on the ground, and let the program take its course with those foolish enough to stand against me. There's no reason why you should deny me twice."

"What about the third option." Aidan's brow was beading with sweat, and his voice grew weak from the last two jolts. "What happens if I break the seal?"

The queen processed the information. "Break the seal, brave adventurer, and then nothing will keep my mighty devils from tearing the flesh from your bones, and no one will get here quick enough to save you."

The floor shifted again, and once more while Aidan and Caro

locked eyes. Her gut wrenched at the pain he was going through, but she knew better than to doubt his resilience and will to win, no matter what the obstacle. She nodded to him as he readied another psychic blast. "I'll take my chances."

The green seal cracked under Aidan's strike and the three devils pounced, two on the psychic and one on the assassin as the lich cast spells to fortify her and her allies' defenses. The devils grew to double their size and the lich encased herself in a stone wall that blocked all avenues of attack. The wall went up just as the first attack from Caro came arcing in. The devils locked in combat with the assassin and psychic and the outer walls began to heat up.

Aidan's psychic earth barriers came up, hitting the two devils at his sides with rocky barrages and sending them toppling backward. Caro hit heavy on the devil in front of her, both of her daggers slicing wildly into the hot flesh. As quickly as one slashing strike made its mark, the previous wound closed. Caro shouted over her shoulder for Aidan to do something, but all he could call back was, "A little busy…" as claw after claw raked toward him. Most of the blows were absorbed by his psychic barriers, but every claw that came through charred his skin as the floors shocked them. The tiles they stood on threatened to cook them, but unless they could fend off the beasts in front of them, they wouldn't make it out of there alive. Aidan noticed through the Plexiglas when the outer door closed, and the walls inside heated up more such that waves of light distorted around them. He wondered how much longer the soundproofing on the walls would hold out before the wood beneath ignited from the electrical fires sizzling behind them.

Caro broke away from the beast that nipped at her. She slid toward Aidan, swinging wildly at the two demons snapping jaws at him and jumping back just out of his reach. She didn't make it to them before catching another claw in her back, as her body started weakening from the rising electrical currents. "I'll distract them. Just do something, ANYTHING."

Aidan took a deep breath and crouched low. He crossed his fingers, then ran up the demon, tipping it until he got five feet above ground. From there, he could see the head of the lich queen behind her iron wall. He loosed every power he held in his magic staff, flooding the database with damage, saving throws, special effects and debilitating statuses. The room went dark, until all they could smell was the smoke hissing from the soundproofed walls.

They sat in breathless silence as the heat dissipated. From the room above them, they heard heavy footsteps coming down the stairs and a slow clapping. Where Caro expected to see Jeb's face, she looked upon Professor Dietrich.

"Well done. You truly are my finest students. The senior and the freshman. I have to admit, though. When I give a multiple choice exam, I don't like it when my pupils make up their own answers."

"Professor Dietrich? What the hell are you doing here? What are you doing running Jeb's missions in the simulator?"

"Ah, yes. Jeb. He's quite an enterprising young man. I told you I keep a close eye on all my students' work, did I not?" He walked down to stand beside the lich queen's immobile corpse. "When I saw his dozens of submissions into the dungeon database, I asked him to create something special as a present for you. When I asked him to make it extra challenging, I don't think he imagined what I had in store for you."

Aidan propped himself up with one arm, weak from the jolts he took to his hands and arms. "You're a sick, sad old man. Is there anything you like more than tormenting little kids?"

"Kids? Ha!" Professor Dietrich moved toward the game master remote and punched in another scenario. "No, I think not. Kids are helpless and weak, and cannot fend for themselves. You have come so far, Mr. Aidan." The lights dimmed slightly as Professor Dietrich punched more buttons into the remote. "You were born to fail, though. You only want a way out, and you refused to take the way up." With a final giggle, he pushed another button to send a shock up through the floorboards into Aidan's body. Aidan convulsed, and then slumped to the floor.

"I must admit, Miss Caro. I was impressed by your Death Certificate project. You solved so many more problems than you realized. I'm afraid I harbor bigger plans for it, however." The smoke thickened as the walls themselves continued to melt. Flames near the entrance licked at the charred walls, growing with every second.

"In the right hands, the dungeon simulator's death certificates can be used to train soldiers in the right and wrong way to perform. Up and coming militias will pay top dollar to use the simulator, and when a soldier is not up to snuff and must be eliminated from the program, your death certificate program will weed them out for us."

He pushed another button and the electrical current arced from the tile below into Aidan, shaking him harder. His feet pushed out, kicking a hole into the wall beside him, revealing red hot conduit charring the boards in the walls.

"Stop!" She pleaded with him, "What can we do? You win. You win," she sobbed. "You can have the whole thing."

"See, I gave you that option, Miss Caro. I handed it to you on a silver platter. Instead, you and your friend here decided to face your devils, and so here I am." He pointed the controller at her, and she felt her hair start to stand on end. As soon as she ran for him, his face hardened as he pushed another button. Electricity stabbed through her back leg from the floor squares, and when her leg straightened she was on another tile, free from the blast. She charged into him, knocking him back into the wall as the controller flew from his hands. At the entryway, a loud crack sounded as firefighters and police swarmed in.

Dr. Dietrich slid to the ground as Caro jumped back, hands held out in helplessness. She stuttered to try and verbalize her innocence, knowing only that they had seen her tackle the unconscious professor. Wordlessly, three police officers rolled him over and cuffed him before dragging him out. She faintly heard a firefighter asking her if she was okay as another turned Aidan over, checking his vitals. She only nodded in nervous confusion as Professor Dietrich was hauled off with his feet dragging behind.

TWENTY-THREE

Chad paced the sidewalk in front of the flashing fire rescue lights, flailing his arms angrily. "You should have called, said something, did something. Hell, you should have done anything to let me know that you needed my help!"

"I'm sorry, Chad." Aidan looked sheepishly at the street below. "I still didn't know if you could be trusted, and we needed to find out for ourselves what was going on in the machine. How were we supposed to know you weren't behind this?"

Chad paced the streets. "How were you supposed to know that I'm not a psychopathic killer who sabotages the best thing that's ever happened to us? Oh, I don't know, because you know that I'm not OUT OF MY MIND."

"So you're saying you're not a psycho?" Caro struggled with two new revelations, only hours apart. The hacking didn't have anything to do with Chad, but that still didn't heal her anger at what she had just found at the house. "How do you explain the ring in your bedroom?"

"You went in my bedroom?" He tried to sound indignant, but he was getting nowhere with her. "Okay, okay. Fine. I stole the ring. I'm a sad, pathetic little man who couldn't get your attention, and so I thought I would be the hero and return something that mattered to you." Caro was so upset, she started crying. "But when I tried to take credit for it at the end of the night, you just shut me out. I tried to get your attention, and when you didn't immediately respond, the moment was gone. I didn't know what else to do, so I held onto it. It was there to remind me that when it counts, sometimes I just shut down."

"Whatever." It didn't sound like an apology, and she really didn't want an apology from him anyway. Caro's phone started to ring. When she looked at it, she wiped the sweat and soot from her brow before answering. "Mom?"

"Jesus, are you alright? The security company called me as soon as the fire alarms went off. What the hell happened?"

"I'm alright. Um, we might have some rebuilding to do."

"That's what insurance is for. I'll see to that."

Evie came running up as Caro finished up her phone call. She ran into Caro's open arms, sobbing heavily. "That was stupid, stupid, stupid. I can't believe you two thought you could do it alone. I can't believe you thought you needed to."

"I don't know what came over me. I guess it was just a spur of the moment, save the day and get all the loot kind of thing." Caro pulled back and took a deep breath. "I'm a self-saving princess, you know. Every once in a while I like to slay the dragon and get the girl."

Evie laughed, "Yeah, well I think my self-saving princess is absolutely crazy," and just as Caro started to pout she added, "...And I'm absolutely crazy about her." She grabbed her by the side of her face and kissed her deeply as the sirens lit up the dim evening city streets. "You are so damn grounded."

The following summer, a tournament was held that brought in game masters from all over the state to compete for the best one-shot missions. The stand-alone modules were put into the system by computer science majors and the results were graded according to difficulty, story and use of special mechanics. The top three were partnered with graduate business students to run the next year's Live Dungeon, and so a business charter was struck so that the business would always be run by students, and the freshest ideas were always implemented into new seasons of play.

After two years of engineering studies, Caro changed her major to theater and performance and landed a dream job soon after, setting up story-building workshops at conventions around the United States. Evie traveled with her when she could, doing freelance photography to keep a little extra money coming in on the side, and while Caro never made the engineering money that she always dreamed would be her ticket out of her small life, she got to travel all over the country and share her own life with throngs of adoring fans who wanted to hear the story of the first-ever immersive gaming dungeon that gave everyone a voice.

She loved that she had done so much more than she set out to do. All she'd wanted was for everyone to hear her story, and instead she gave thousands of people the means to tell their own.

About the Author

Jeff Babineaux grew up in southern Louisiana where Cajun culture takes great pride in folklore and the ability to pass these tales along. This love inspires narratives rich in the assertion that everyone has a story, and should be afforded the platform to share it. Jeff's goal as a literary guide is to introduce worlds and characters that are relatable and yet live outside of rules that convince us to keep quiet and color in the lines.

When he isn't taking his turn as game master at the table, Jeff enjoys improvising recipes in the kitchen, wooing the woman of his dreams, and pursuing a career in electrical engineering.

www.ingramcontent.com/pod-product-compliance
Lightning Source LLC
Chambersburg PA
CBHW060141130626
46556CB00006B/2440